MYSTERY CASE FILES

"I need to see Detective Chief Inspector Paddington."

The assistant pushed her glasses up with an index finger. "He's busy, Mrs. Graham."

"It's critical that I speak to someone. You see, I found—"

"The D.C.I. will get to you when he has a moment, flower. Or you can return when—"

Molly couldn't stand it anymore. "Can I use a phone? Please?"

The assistant gestured to a desk overflowing with papers and used foam cups. "You can use that one."

Molly was quick to punch in the numbers. "Michael. No, I'm not using my mobile. It fell off the side of the cliff where I was hiking. I'd pulled it out to call you and the D.C.I., but I dropped it."

"Molly, are you all right? You sound upset," Michael said.

"I'm fine, really. It's just... I'm at the police station...to report a dead body."

Cast of Characters

Michael and Molly Graham—The young couple have come to Blackpool for a simpler life... Only, things in the small town are anything but simple.

D.C.I. Paddington—The stolid inspector has a laid-back approach to investigation—so laid-back that it's fuelled rumors he's only in Blackpool to bide his time until retirement.

The Crowes—The members of the Crowe family are reputed to have more secrets than they have money. And they keep both very well.

Dennis Carteret and Percy Lethbridge— The two men are members of the planning board for Blackpool's harbor renovation—but they hadn't planned on a conspiracy.

Rosamund Carteret—Dennis's only child, and his world. The teenager lost her mother when she was very young, and Dennis would do *anything* to shield her from further suffering.

Francis Weymouth—He says his only ambition is to protect the environment, though he seems awfully cozy with the media. And very antagonistic toward Molly.

Rohan Wallace—The Jamaican émigré came to Blackpool to work, but lately he and Michael have become obsessed with the legend of Charles Crowe's stolen gypsy gold. Is his interest purely recreational?

Greed, jealousy, betrayal, trickery, murder— secrets are the heart of Blackpool.

MYSTERY CASE FILES

Submerged

A BLACKPOOL MYSTERY

Jordan Gray

HARLEQUIN®

TORONTO • NEW YORK • LONDON
AMSTERDAM • PARIS • SYDNEY • HAMBURG
STOCKHOLM • ATHENS • TOKYO • MILAN • MADRID
PRAGUE • WARSAW • BUDAPEST • AUCKLAND

Special thanks and acknowledgment to Jean Rabe for her contribution to this work.

This one's for Vicki, who says she will never wear a red hat, but I have seen her wear purple.

Recycling programs
for this product may
not exist in your area.

ISBN-13: 978-0-373-83753-3

SUBMERGED

Copyright © 2011 by Harlequin Books S.A.

www.eHarlequin.com

Printed in U.S.A.

CHAPTER ONE

MOLLY GRAHAM CAME TO a shaky stop in front of an old Victorian on Walnut Grove, steeling herself to go inside Blackpool's police station. Except for the modest sign near the walk, a passerby wouldn't have thought it anything other than a stately old house with a primrose garden in need of serious weeding. The white paint was peeling in places around the cornices on the second floor.

In contrast, the inside was completely modern, though nothing she would call "state of the art." There was a drop ceiling in the main room, and fluorescent lights hung from it. The air was filled with the scent of lavender and Lysol, and an underlying acrid pong of cigarette smoke. Not that anyone could smoke in the building, but she knew that a scattering of officers and assistants did so elsewhere, and the odor clung to their clothes.

The assistant at the front desk—the only person Molly spotted this afternoon—was a petite woman who would have been forced into retirement years ago, had she been with a larger city's police department. She looked at Molly through wire-rimmed trifocals, tucked a few wisps of iron-gray hair behind one ear and waited for Molly to speak.

Molly drew a calming breath. "I need to see Detective Chief Inspector Paddington."

The woman pushed her glasses up with an index finger. "He's busy, Mrs. Graham."

Although Molly didn't know the woman, she wasn't surprised the assistant recognized her; Molly had her picture in the newspaper enough times, especially recently. She wished it had more to do with the grants that she had helped to secure for the town, but to Molly and her husband, Michael's, dismay, their notoriety seemed to stem from a series of local murders and mysteries that they had solved—which brought Molly back to why she was here.

"This is very important."

"I'm sure it is."

"Please, can you tell him—"

"Is it a life-and-death emergency?"

"Yes." A pause. "Well, not exactly, but—"

"Then take a seat, flower, and he'll get to you when he has time."

Trying to find some composure, Molly brushed her fingers along the edge of the desk. It was walnut, with a heavy lacquer on it, handmade by a craftsman and not mass-produced in some factory like the rest of the desks in the small department. She wondered if it had come with the house when the city bought it for the station.

"How about Sergeant Krebs? I could talk to her."

"You could if she wasn't busy, too." The woman made a huffing sound. "They're both occupied because of *you*, Mrs. Graham. They're in a meeting about tomorrow's big marina to-do."

"It's critical that I speak to someone. You see, I found—"

"I'm sure it is. Everything you do is momentous, isn't it, Mrs. Graham? But I'm sure this is nothing that can't wait, eh?"

Molly felt a surge of panic. "How about another officer? I don't care which one, but—"

The woman shook her head and eased back from her desk. The glasses had slid halfway down her nose, and she pushed them up again. "The D.C.I. will get to you when he has a moment, flower. Or you can return when—"

Molly couldn't stand it anymore. "Can I use a phone? Please."

The assistant gestured to a desk overflowing with papers and used foam cups. The tag on it read Sergeant Merle Oates. "You can use that one…if it's a local call."

Molly was quick to punch in the numbers. She tapped her fingers on the only empty spot on the desk. "C'mon, c'mon. Iris? Put Michael on." She drummed faster. "Michael? No, I'm not using my mobile. It fell off the side of the cliff where I was hiking. I'd pulled it out to call you and the D.C.I., but I dropped it."

"Molly, are you all right? You sound upset," Michael said.

"I'm fine, really. It's just…I'm at the police station… to report a dead body." Molly noticed the old woman quickly pick up her own phone. "I'm going back out there to try to figure out who it is and what happened. I should've done that right away, I guess, poked around, but I didn't want to disturb anything before the police looked it over."

"What? A body? Molly, slow down—"

"I didn't get that close, but I think he must have slipped and cracked his head open on a rock. It isn't an easy hiking trail, you know, even for a young person in good shape. Paddington's too busy right now to deal with it so I'm going back on my own."

"No, don't go by yourself. I'll meet you there. Where is it?" Michael asked.

Relief flooded over her. "It's out by Jack Hawkins's nose. See you soon, love."

Molly raced out the front door, feet flying down the steps. She slid into her car just as D.C.I. Paddington and Sergeant Krebs ran out a side door.

"Molly!" Paddington waved at her. "Wait, Molly!"

She had the top down on her Mini Cooper, and she twisted in the seat toward him.

"What's this about reporting a murder?" Paddington demanded.

Gripping the car, he loomed over her. Krebs, half

his age and size, stayed a step back and regarded her reflection in the Mini Cooper's gloss paint.

"A dead body," Molly corrected. "I was hiking—"

"—out by Hawkins's nose," Krebs interrupted. "That's what Evelyn told us."

Paddington raised a bushy eyebrow at Krebs.

"Yes, that's where I was." Molly started the car. "Follow me, I'll show you. I believe the man slipped. Like I told Michael, it's not an easy trail, and it's not well marked."

Paddington nodded and turned toward a nearby police cruiser, Krebs not far behind. Molly eased away from the curb, not waiting for Paddington to change his mind and order her to stay away.

She kept the top down, even though it felt a little chilly this late in the afternoon. The car had been a gift from Michael last year, and it gave her comfort as she drove toward the horror she'd discovered earlier.

Molly kept to the speed limit, no easy feat. But she needed to give Paddington and Krebs a chance to catch up. Besides, the dead body wasn't going anywhere. As Molly headed down Walnut Grove and turned on Main, she noticed a police cruiser pull up behind her; it looked like Krebs was driving—no flashers or siren.

They wound their way to the southern outskirts of Blackpool and onto an access road that ran along the cliffs.

Molly often found excuses to drive this road during the late spring because of the colors—leaves greening

and flowers springing up everywhere. That's why she'd
gone hiking this afternoon. It had been too lovely to
pass the time indoors. That, and she wanted a distraction to keep her mind off tomorrow's groundbreaking
ceremony for the harbor renovation.

She considered this part of the countryside especially stunning. From here it looked like all of Blackpool was a watercolor painting and the buildings, with
their colorful red roofs, seemed to be tumbling down
the cobbled streets toward the sea.

After a few more minutes she pulled onto a narrow
strip of gravel and waited for the cruiser to stop behind
her, trying not to think about what awaited them. She
got out and walked toward the edge of the cliff. The
sun, just starting to set, turned the waves a glimmering
copper down below.

"What were you doing way out here?" The question
came from Krebs, who had silently appeared behind
her. The policewoman verged on petite, but she had
a masculine look about her, with a square jaw and
short-cropped hair.

"To enjoy the day and St. Hilda's Serpents," Molly
answered.

"Fossils," Paddington explained, joining them.
"Blackpool has one of the richest coasts for fossils on
the north shore of England."

Krebs snorted. "Fossils."

Ignoring her, Paddington continued. "At low tide
in the rock pools, coiled ammonites, nicknamed St.

Hilda's Serpents, can be found. I used to look myself once in a while…but in places where the trails are a little friendlier."

Molly heard the approach of a motorcycle and spun to see Michael pull up.

"Wonderful," Krebs growled. "Might as well invite the whole town."

"Afternoon, Michael," Paddington greeted, then turned to Molly. "Show me this dead body. I want to take a look before I call the coroner. Hopefully we can get this wrapped up before we lose the light."

"Is anyone else joining us?" Krebs asked Molly. "Did you invite more people, Mrs. Graham?"

Molly didn't bother to answer. She started picking her way down the side of the cliff, pointing to her left and right at narrow spots they should avoid.

There were only a few handrails along this trail. In her opinion they marred the scenery, but made it a little safer for the less surefooted hikers—and now the police.

Michael nimbly stepped around Paddington and joined Molly. Experienced hikers, the Grahams were familiar with the long, winding trails that cut across the entire coastline, including this section.

The handrails stopped when the trail became steeper, discouraging the less proficient hikers from going further.

"Pretty desolate here," Michael observed.

"And beautiful," Molly added. There were a few

cottages along the ridge farther to the south, and soft glows came from some of the windows. The air was clean here, and the wind carried a slight chill. It smelled of salt and rocks and felt good against her face.

"Careful," Michael cautioned Paddington.

The D.C.I. motioned for Krebs to stay behind him. "Two more years," he grumbled. "Two more bloody years."

"Not much farther!" Molly called several minutes later.

"What!" Paddington said. "If we keep going we'll be in the sea."

"Here." Molly stopped on a meter-wide ledge and pointed. "He's down there, see?"

"Not yet," Paddington said.

Michael maneuvered around Molly so they were out of the D.C.I.'s way.

"Should've called Oates to handle this." Paddington leaned over and peered at the rocky terrain below and a thin strip of rock covered with scree. "Is that a footprint? It's as dry as Ghandi's flip-flop here. Hasn't rained in days." He took a few more steps down and reached out a hand as if to catch himself. "I'll probably take a tumble and ice myself, and you berks will be left with Krebs."

Molly quietly watched him as she inched forward. She noticed Krebs was staying farther up on what passed for a trail. "See him yet?"

There was a shuffling sound, the *click-click-click* of a rock caroming down the cliff from Paddington's movements. Nobody else even breathed, and the sounds around Molly seemed to intensify—the lapping of the sea against the base of the cliff, the cry of some bird, farther away was the shushing sound of a car driving by up on the main road, and fainter came a dog barking.

"Yes, I see the poor bloke," Paddington finally said. "Now, how the hell am I going to get to him?" He looked up. "Sergeant Krebs...call it in and notify the coroner."

The D.C.I. managed to get on his hands and knees and lever himself over the edge of the cliff. Molly and Michael joined him and hovered, hands out to grab him if it looked as if he was going to slip.

Paddington scrambled onto the lower ledge. "And Krebs? Get Oates out here and tell him to bring some ropes with him." Molly started down the last section just as he added, "You two, stay there."

Seconds later when she knelt beside him, he shook a scolding finger at her. "I thought I ordered you to keep back."

"Sorry."

"Jack Hawkins's nose, eh?"

She nodded to a long, bulbous rocky outcropping that shadowed the body.

"The actor from Middlesex," Michael explained. He stayed on the rocks above them, recognizing there was not enough space for all of them. "He was in *Lawrence of Arabia, Ben-Hur, Zulu, The Bridge on the River Kwai...*"

Molly was shoulder-to-shoulder with Paddington, and now could see the body clearly. The dead man had looked elderly to her, but she hadn't been that close when she'd first spotted him. Now she realized that he was quite young, and she'd been confused by the rock dust on his skin and all the bruises. His clothes were rumpled and torn from the fall, his legs and arms twisted, and already the hungry, curious sea birds had inflicted damage on his body. She wrinkled her nose at the foul stench and sucked in a breath when she spotted a small crab crawl out of his mouth and scurry away.

"I'd say late twenties," Paddington said. "Maybe thirty, but no older than that." If the odor bothered Paddington, he didn't let it show. "Tennis shoes."

New-looking ones, Molly noted, but a cheap brand. Molly knew shoes. "Not what I'd wear to hike this cliff," she remarked. Actually, not what she'd ever wear.

"Been dead two, three days, I'd wager."

"That recent?" Molly was surprised by Paddington's assessment. The body looked so decomposed she would have thought it had been here weeks or months.

"But how—"

"The sea air," Paddington explained as he pulled a pen out and used it to open the flap of the dead man's shirt pocket and fish around inside. "Bodies decay fast in the open. The salt, the water spraying up here, the birds and crabs, other scavengers. Two days, maybe three at the outside, but the coroner will tell us for sure. Poor bloke." He searched the other pocket. "Empty. Figures."

Molly stared at the top of the corpse's head. That way she could avoid looking into its empty eye sockets. She'd read somewhere that birds went for the eyes first. "All this blood..." she said. "I figured he had been hiking and fell, hit his head." The rock beneath the body was stained dark. She suspected there'd been more blood, but the sea spray had no doubt washed some of it away.

After pulling on gloves, Paddington gently examined the corpse's skull. "Oh, he hit his head all right, and broke a few other bones in the process. But he was dead before that." He pointed to the man's neck, moving the shirt collar open and exposing the jagged line across the man's throat.

Molly felt bile rising in her mouth when she tried looking away and her gaze passed over the eye sockets again. Maybe it hadn't been such a good idea, climbing down here with the D.C.I. Maybe she should have just given him directions.

"Slit all the way across," Paddington pronounced. "*That's* what killed him. This young fellow was murdered." He angled around to the other side of the body and shifted it to check the pants' pockets.

"No wallet, no ID, a couple of folded euros and a

green tin of chewing tobacco." He straightened and regarded Molly. "Maybe he wasn't carrying a wallet. Or maybe the killer took it."

"So you don't know who he was."

"No." Paddington turned to stare out to sea. "But I'll make short work of it, no doubt. It'll give me something to do…not that I need anything else with that big marina to-do of yours tomorrow. It's going to be quite the show, I'm sure…."

CHAPTER TWO

MOLLY COULDN'T SMELL the fish, though she normally smelled nothing but when she came to the marina.

Today, the perfumes and aftershaves of the crowd overpowered any hint of fish, though Molly could still detect the scent of sizzling bacon from a dockside café still serving breakfast and a sudden belch of diesel fumes from a tourist bus that had pulled up.

The sounds were almost as overwhelming as the smells. The radio on the bus blared Topley-Bird's vocals on Massive Attack's "Psyche." The chatter of people moving past her sounded like swarms of insects, their monotone buzzing interspersed with the bass bleat of a tugboat out in the harbor. In the distance came the wail of an ambulance siren.

Molly raised her eyes to appreciate the fine weather, the bright sky full of beggar gulls. It was a perfect day for the official groundbreaking—the few clouds thin and high with no hint of rain. The pleasant temperature had helped to lure much of the town to this spot for the ceremony that would officially announce a major overhaul of the harbor. Molly had written the grant proposals to secure the funds, and was excited to see the work begin.

Beside her, Michael was clearly not as enrapt. Her husband was talking into his mobile about the computer game he was designing, something called "Dead Space."

"Michael, can't you put work aside for just a little while?" Molly tugged on his arm and steered him through a group of red-hatted ladies who were all on the far side of middle age.

"Hold a moment, please," he said into the phone. He winked at her. "*I* shouldn't work? You're working." A boyish expression spread across his handsome face. He waved his free arm to encompass the gathering on the dock. "You'll be working most of the day."

"Well…yes…sort of," she reluctantly admitted. "Though I'd rather be looking into the murder."

"Grisly pastime that. I think I'd rather you be here, appreciating the results of all your efforts. Admit it, you're chuffed to bits by all of this."

Molly had to agree that she was pleased. But she also wished this event was next week, not today. While she was happy about these festivities, her curiosity about the dead man was eating at her. She wanted to be talking to people who lived in the area about the murdered man's identity, maybe fishermen who might have seen him on the cliff…and who might also have spotted his killer.

But she did have a right to be proud today. The

buzzing crowds were turning Blackpool's docks into a carnival atmosphere and it was largely because of her. She didn't object to standing in the spotlight, and actually relished being the center of attention from time to time. It made her feel necessary, and she liked to think she was leaving her mark on the world, something to indicate she'd made a difference.

Michael ended his phone conversation, promising to call back someone named Alvin to discuss the effects of faster-than-light travel on zombie astronauts. He stuffed the iPhone in his front pocket. "You're practically glowing," he said. "You put Lily Donaldson to shame today, Molly."

Molly struggled to avoid smiling. Inwardly she beamed at being compared to a young British supermodel. "I'll never be that skinny," she protested.

"Lord, I wouldn't want you to. You're perfect the way you are."

Molly had put extra effort into her appearance this morning. She'd had her hair and makeup done at seven, the stylist opening an hour early to accommodate her, and she wore a new ivory-colored blouse over dark green pants that Iris had pressed, so a faultless crease ran down the front. She carried a light tweed jacket and a new leather handbag was looped over her shoulder. It matched the shoes that she'd been wearing around the house for a few days to break them in.

She'd kept the jewelry simple: a black onyx set in a pendant hung from a fine silver chain around her neck; small hoop earrings, difficult to see beneath her hair; her wedding ring, of course, and on the other hand a pearl set in a bronze twist that fit her index finger. They were among her favorite pieces, and she considered them lucky.

She wanted positive coverage from the reporters. At least they'd be concentrating fully on the marina, since Paddington had released nothing yet about the murder. She knew there would be some media in attendance, scattered throughout the harbor, and she hoped to look her best—but not overdone—on camera. Business-casual, they called it in the States. Michael, however, was wearing casual-casual, new jeans and a polo shirt.

"I don't think I've ever been in such a crowd," he continued. "Well, at least not in Blackpool. See what you have wrought, Molly!"

Molly's background in public relations and grant writing had served Blackpool well on a few previous occasions, but she'd outdone herself this time by landing an impressive government-administered "green grant" that would cover a good portion of renovation to the town's docks and marina. She'd secured some matching local pledges, too, including a hefty one she and Michael had put up. The planning committee was responsible for the project now, but Molly's name was still very much attached to it in the news coverage.

"I wonder how long it will take the D.C.I. to learn who that man was," she mused to Michael.

"It'll take as long as it takes," Michael said, keeping his voice low. "Paddington's pretty efficient. I have to admit, though, I would rather be poking around about the murder than here rubbing shoulders with the local officials and media."

Not only had this event caught the attention of regional newspapers, as well as magazines and television stations, but rumor also had it that someone from the History Channel would be filming.

"Good thing the reporters haven't heard about the dead man. Let them concentrate on your grants, Molly."

"Focus on good news for a change, huh?" Molly scanned the crowd. She recognized people everywhere she turned. They were dressed informally for the most part, though she could see that the planning board members, town councilmen, business owners and the like had taken their appearance up a notch because of all the cameras.

There were tourists as well, like the group who'd filed off the bus.

And then there were the Gypsies. Her stomach twisted into a knot when she spied a group of them on the dock. They weren't wearing coin belts and scarflike skirts or carrying tambourines as the movies portrayed them. In fact, they could have passed for tourists were it not for their exaggerated, mismatched garb, long hair, gold hoop earrings and swarthy complexions.

They were relatively new to Blackpool, and rumor

had it that they were after the gold that the town's founder, Charles Crowe, had stolen from their ancestors. The tallest one, who was about six feet, walked with a swagger and gestured wildly.

His name was Stefan Draghici, and she'd heard from the town gossips that he was the head of the family that was staying in Blackpool. His hair, cascading in coarse curls down to the middle of his back, was as dark as his eyes. Not a trace of gray in it, though she guessed him to be in his fifties. Draghici's two sons and his wife must be nearby. She saw his daughter, Anjeza, dressed provocatively and drawing stares from Blackpool's young men. The girl was, indeed, beautiful. The family reminded Molly of bloodhounds hot on a scent, though she wondered if the gold they were after really existed.

Well, they weren't going to find any gold on the docks. But they'd certainly get publicity if they wanted it.

Michael noticed the focus of her attention. "Easy," he said. "The Draghicis are probably down here to see what's going on. Just like everyone else."

"Yeah, I suppose. But I doubt they're really in town for the groundbreaking." She sidestepped a group of the red-hatted ladies, all of them dressed in varying shades of purple and wearing buttons proclaiming themselves the Brighton Belles.

"There she is!" shouted a silver-haired man with

a camera perched on his shoulder. "There's Molly Graham!"

A young woman holding a microphone shouldered her way past him and headed straight toward Molly. The reporter was dressed in a pale blue suit and had dark red lipstick that made Molly think she'd been sucking on a cherry Popsicle.

She swung to Molly's side, held up the mike and adjusted her hair. "Jennessee Stanwood with Channel M of the Guardian Media Group, reporting live from Blackpool." Jennessee stared straight into the camera.

Channel M was out of Manchester. Not one of the major stations there. Still, it was significant that they'd sent someone to cover the ceremony.

She tried to read the numbers and letters on the other cameras in the mix and spied an older reporter talking to one of the Blackpool planning board members a few yards away. With all the noise she couldn't catch what they were saying.

"With me is Molly Graham, the woman who landed the grant to cover this renovation of the town's historic and notorious harbor." Jennessee droned on for another few moments, and then turned slightly to Molly, holding the microphone just under her chin. "Can you tell us why, Mrs. Graham, you've spent so much time working on this grant? I understand you were not paid to do this, and that you personally won't make any profit from the construction."

Molly saw Michael inch away, heading toward the café while pulling his iPhone out of his pocket, no doubt to talk about space-faring undead.

"I love Blackpool," Molly began, "and I have experience going after grants. This one…"

"Six hundred and fifty thousand pounds, correct? And some matching local money on top of that?"

Molly nodded. "Which certainly will not cover everything, but will ensure that the history of the marina is preserved, keeping the original construction of the buildings intact, down to the hardwood floors, fixtures, tin ceilings in some cases. At the same time, we're protecting the ecological integrity of the harbor, the whole wharf area. It's an ambitious plan that—"

"Preserve history?" The voice cut loudly above the various conversations that floated in the air. "Preserve history?" The crowd quieted.

Molly couldn't see the speaker at first, but a few heartbeats later he shouldered his way through the throng, the red-hatted ladies parting like the Red Sea to allow him passage.

It was Barnaby Stone, who owned a bait-and-tackle shop on the wharf.

"You're not preserving anything, Molly Graham!"

The cameraman spun to record Barnaby, red-faced and shaking his fist. He had come dressed for the event in worn blue jeans and a bright yellow T-shirt with "Barnaby's Bait" emblazoned in black letters on it.

Molly's shoulders slumped. Barnaby had been one of the project's opponents in the town meetings, but he'd never been this vocal.

The reporter stepped away from Molly and toward Barnaby, holding the microphone out.

"So much for focusing on the good news for a change," Molly grumbled.

Other reporters jockeyed to get closer to Barnaby.

Jennessee smiled sweetly. "Could you tell us, Mr.—"

Barnaby didn't give her a chance to finish the sentence. He plowed on with his rant, the camera getting every juicy word and catching every piece of spittle that flew from his bulbous lips.

"Ecology? Preserving history?" He stomped his foot and raised his fist higher.

Out of the corner of her eye, Molly noticed three planning board members trying to weave their way through the press of bodies. Farther back, a constable was angling toward them.

Hurry, she thought. *Get Barnaby to shut up.* It wasn't her place to intervene, nor was she interested in a public debate. That had already occurred in board meetings.

"Ecology has nothing to do with this," Barnaby continued. "It's pounds from the tourists—that's what this is all about. And tourists don't buy enough of my bait to put food on my table." He sucked in a deep breath. "This construction is going to put me out of business.

That damn grant doesn't cover the whole cost. I have to shell out from my own pockets. We all do! It'll put a load of us under and our livelihoods down the loo."

Jennessee tried to ask a question, but Barnaby kept going.

"A cancer is what Molly Graham has brought to Blackpool!"

"He's right!" cried another business owner. "A cancer that will spread and kill us all."

A prune of a woman shouldered her way into the mix. Miss Alice Coffey, Molly recognized with chagrin. The woman was the head of the August Historical Preservation Society, which—flip a coin—was alternately for and against the marina renovation. Most recently against—after Alice had met with Aleister Crowe.

Miss Coffey said something, but it couldn't be heard above the ruckus.

"Go back to America!" someone hollered. "We don't want your kind of help, Molly Graham."

"Go back to New York! Get that city a green grant, why don't you! That cesspool needs it more than Blackpool."

A few cameras whirled to catch Molly's reaction.

She stood dumbstruck, tweed jacket sliding off her arm and landing at her feet.

"Go back! Go back!" Someone tried to start a chant.

"This is Jennessee Stanwood with Channel M of

the Guardian Media Group, reporting from Black-pool." The reporter had to raise her voice. "What was supposed to be a pleasant groundbreaking ceremony has become a shouting match between grant-writer Molly Graham and local businesspeople who feel the renovations are being rammed down their collective throats. This pretty day has turned ugly and erupted into—"

As if on cue, a scream pierced the air. It was punctu-ated by a thrown punch and someone hitting the ground like a tossed sack of potatoes. The press of bodies was so tight Molly couldn't see who was involved.

Another punch. More fleshy thuds, followed by more screams, panicked shouts and whoops of en-couragement for whomever was joining in the fight.

The board members forced their way through the crowd.

Molly thought everyone would have scattered, but instead, people shifted to form a human ring, backing up just enough to accommodate the combatants and the press recording it all for posterity. The red-hatted ladies struggled to get a front-row view.

The Draghici family moved in closer, too, the clan leader keeping an eye on his daughter, who was posing for a young man with a cell-phone camera.

The dockworkers had stopped what they were doing and joined the audience. Waitresses were coming out of the café, Michael with them, scanning the crowd.

"Molly! Molly!" The rest of his words were lost in the cheers and boos and piercing sirens.

Michael's words of several minutes ago echoed in her mind:

See what you have wrought, Molly!

CHAPTER THREE

"OH, WHY COULDN'T THIS BE happening next week instead?" Molly said. She'd rather be poking into the murder of the young man on the cliffs, not facing this angry horde.

The pros and cons of the marina project had been hashed out already; Molly had witnessed most of the meetings and answered the barrage of questions about what costs the grant would cover. Blackpool's council was a unitary authority form of government, and as such, the council oversaw housing, tax collection, education, libraries and municipal projects, and set up boards to deal with specific matters. Such as the wharf renovation.

The planning board members had been appointed by the council many months ago and were accountable to it. They'd held several public meetings, attentively listening to concerns about the proposed construction and harbor work, the latter of which included a good bit of dredging to deepen the channel. They'd even met with the August Historical Preservation Society.

All the board members, the historical society—at the time—and the majority of citizens agreed the pros of the project very much outweighed the cons. So after six months of study, the board had recommended that the project go ahead, the council's gavel sounded and Molly went after the grant from the nation's Sustainable Development Fund. She knew several "green grants" were available, was an expert at writing proposals and thought it was the least she could do for her new hometown.

And though the dissenters had continued to quietly grumble, Molly had assumed that all of the public naysaying had been swept under the proverbial rug.

But Barnaby had tossed that rug out the window a few minutes ago…along with any chance of favorable coverage on the evening news. His wasn't the only shop affected along the wharf. Grandage's Bait and Tackle was larger and in better shape, did a more profitable business and the owner, Jamey Grandage, championed the renovation. Why couldn't Barnaby see that his own business might actually improve because of the renovations?

She tried to back away from the crowds, managing to find some breathing room as she put space between herself and the throng of people. The whole gathering reminded her of an amateur boxing match. The punches thrown were clumsy, and it was difficult to tell who was on which side of the argument as more and more spectators got involved.

She spotted her expensive tweed jacket being trampled by a teenager jostling for a better view of the brawl, a fitting metaphor for her hope and excitement about the project.

Faintly, she heard the cry "Go home, Molly Graham," and she knew the man didn't mean to her manor house on the outskirts of Blackpool.

"I'm an outsider here, too, dear heart." Michael had found her and pulled her even farther away from the melee. Michael was British through and through, but he hailed from London. Not quite an "outsider" like Molly, he was nonetheless not considered a local. Blackpoolers were a tight community. "Maybe this was all a mistake."

She understood he didn't mean the harbor project.

"No," she said. "I like it here, I really do. Our house. The people. And they don't all hate me."

"*Us.* No, they don't all hate *us.*" He smelled of bacon and she inhaled deeply, finding the scent oddly reassuring at the moment.

"Most of them are quite friendly actually."

Michael laughed and put his arm around her shoulders, drawing her close. "The friendly ones just aren't as vocal this morning, eh? The nutters are the loud blokes."

"Nutters?"

"All right, Barnaby passed nutter and went straight to barmy."

"I thought I was doing something worthwhile here," she said, more to herself than to Michael. "The harbor needed—"

"A sprucing? It certainly does." He leaned over and kissed the top of her head. "We wouldn't have personally contributed so heavily if it wasn't warranted. And you *are* doing a good thing here. Barnaby's just getting his fifteen minutes of fame."

"Venting his steam—that's what he's doing," said another man behind them. It was Percy Lethbridge. Molly had spotted him earlier with two other planning board members. His companions were working their way through the ring of spectators, trying to reach Barnaby, who appeared to have acquired a broken nose. Blood splattered his once-bright yellow shirt. "I think he had too much to drink last night, Molly, and this is all the product of a hangover." Softer, so only she could hear, he added, "There's something I need to talk to you about. But not here, and not now."

"Later then," she said.

"When we've a little more privacy. When there's no Barnaby Stone bellowing about."

"I sympathize with him, Percy," she said. "Barnaby has to kick in a good bit of money of his own, but—"

A cheer went up and Molly spotted one of the combatants drop. "Good lord."

A shrill whistle cut above the shouts and a constable shouldered his way through. Someone in the crowd started whistling back, and there were guffaws and more cheers. Molly saw another constable, and at the edge of the gathering D.C.I. Paddington. The Draghici family moved farther away from the police, as Stefan headed onto the largest dock.

A head above the mass, Molly caught sight of Aleister Crowe. He was perched on something. In his mid-thirties, he was only a handful of years older than her and Michael. His dark hair was slicked back, making his widow's peak prominent.

He reminded her of a vulture, both predatory and scavenger, looming over the carnage and surveying people with eyes set close over a beaklike nose. The sunlight glinted off the silver crow's head that topped his walking stick. He waved it and shouted, though she couldn't hear what he was saying. The noise was deafening, and she realized she couldn't really make any of it out—it was just a wall of sound closing in on her.

There were more whistles from the constables, a long sustained blast from Paddington and, miraculously, the crowd quieted. The D.C.I. obviously commanded respect from the locals.

"Go home, Molly Graham!" It was Barnaby, who had been nabbed by one of the constables, hands cuffed behind him. A man with an equally bloody shirt was also being detained, the pair of them prodded toward a police van. "Go home, I say!"

"I have to go, Molly. But we must talk soon." Lethbridge gave Molly's arm a gentle squeeze and strode toward Paddington. "Calm down, everyone!" He gestured like a conductor. "The show is over. Calm down."

Crowe was now talking animatedly to Jennessee and had climbed down from his perch. He pointed to a building behind him: Nan's Nautical Inn, an eatery that belonged to Dennis Carteret, who also served on the planning board. It was the first building to be renovated and work had already begun. Carteret was only a few yards away, trying to quiet the Brighton Belles.

"Molly? Molly Graham?"

She'd been so distracted watching Crowe that she hadn't seen another newsman approach her. He was short, maybe five-five or five-six, with broad swimmer's shoulders and a face weathered by the sun. Good-looking, though, and with a strong voice that must carry well on television.

"Yes, I'm Molly Graham."

"Garrison Headly with BBC Four." He held the microphone toward her. Behind him a cameraman magically appeared. "Mrs. Graham, you're responsible for acquiring the green grant that made this project possible?"

Molly didn't say anything. She was still a little numb from watching the fight.

"It's a considerable grant, is that correct?"

She blinked. "Yes."

The reporter started to become flustered; she wasn't giving him anything for his piece.

"Mrs. Graham, how is the grant money being

administered? Do you decide which businesses are entitled to—"

"No. It's the planning board," she said, squaring her shoulders. "The members of the planning board were appointed by the town council to oversee the project. The board allocates the grant money to the various businesses and to the company that will be doing the dredging work out in the harbor. I only obtained the grant and organized the local contributions. I've also applied for a few more, so hopefully less will have to be paid by the individual business owners. But how it's all divided is not up to me." She locked eyes with the reporter. "The merits of the project—"

"I understand that you and your husband made a sizable contribution."

She nodded. If he wanted to know the amount, he could ferret that out from the planning board's open records.

"The grant…how did you obtain it?"

She let out a breath, the curls fluttering against her forehead. "I knew that grant money was available from the Sustainable Development Fund. Normally home owners and small businesses apply for individual grants, but there are exceptions for larger projects such as this. I was able to demonstrate the need for the work, and the fact that the harbor is steeped in history and that the business owners wanted to preserve as much of the original—"

"*Most* of the business owners, from what I

understand," Headly interrupted. "There are a few exceptions, as we noted just a handful of minutes ago. The owner of the bait shop, for example."

Molly inclined her head slightly, her eyes daggers. "*One* of the bait shops," she corrected.

"But some of the owners are afraid they are actually going to lose the history of the wharf section, not have it preserved. Could you explain—"

"That's not true. The grant would not have been awarded if we hadn't planned to retain the history of this place," Molly protested. But over the next several minutes as Headly continued to grill her, it was clear he was focused only on the conflict. Michael stayed within arm's reach the entire time, and she wondered if he'd become as tired of all of this as she had.

She'd honestly thought obtaining the grant was a good idea.

She wouldn't have spent the time and energy on it otherwise. She could have curled up in an easy chair with a stack of mystery books and pleasantly wiled away the days instead of writing the thick proposal, staying up until all hours doing the research and preparing the presentation.

Maybe she shouldn't have gotten involved with the marina work, she thought now. Maybe the project should have been left to the locals, the native Blackpoolers who treasured their close-knit community.

But without the grant she'd obtained, only half of the proposed work would have been possible. In that case, many buildings, like Barnaby's Bait Shop, would have continued to fall apart, victim to the salty sea air and age. On the other hand, Grandage would have been more than happy to lose what little competition Barnaby's business provided.

Her bleak mood was reflected in the reporter's closing comments. "So despite the pronounced opposition, Molly Graham forged ahead and obtained an impressive grant to refurbish this town's historic and notorious harbor," Headly concluded. "Molly, an American, is married to world-renowned computer game designer Michael Graham. They chose to settle in this peaceful coastal town, which is anything but today. This is Garrison Headly, reporting from Blackpool."

CHAPTER FOUR

MICHAEL TUGGED HER toward the café.

"My jacket—"

"I'm afraid it's been trampled, love. C'mon. It'll be a little less noisy in here. You'll still be close enough, and when this rabble clears and the ceremony actually starts, you can run right out there and smile for the cameras."

She groaned but didn't protest.

"Besides, Molly, my love, they have excellent breakfast."

"Isn't it a little late for that? And didn't you already eat when I was getting my hair done? You're like a hobbit—you want a second breakfast."

He escorted her graciously through the door. "Yes, and yes," he replied. "But I didn't have much the first time, just a muffin, and they're serving brunch, actually…omelets filled with cheddar, and bangers. And I'm still hungry."

Molly wrinkled her nose.

"The bangers aren't too spicy here. I promise."

There was only one empty table. Molly sat facing

the front so she could stare out at the dissipating bedlam.

Michael nudged the menu toward her. "Bloody Marys, too. Made from scratch, they claim."

Molly glanced at the offerings. Her stomach rumbled, but she didn't have much of an appetite. "I'll have a yogurt."

Michael's mobile chirped but he ignored it, stuffing it farther down in his pocket to muffle the sound.

"Don't you need to answer that? To deal with your vampires in orbit and whatnot?" Her attempt at humor was forced. "Mummies on meteors?"

He reached across the table and gently squeezed her hand. A waitress hovered, tapping her pen against her order pad.

"The omelet with the bangers, extra cheddar," he said. "Pineapple juice for both of us, a yogurt for Molly."

"Plain?" the waitress asked.

"Strawberry if you have it," Molly answered.

The woman walked away, bobbing her head and tapping her pen.

Molly relaxed, but only a little. The smells in the cozy café were preferable to the assault on her senses outside. Cinnamon, bacon, oranges—together they made a pleasing combination. The conversations were more subdued, some purposely hushed, she was sure. But she easily picked up the theme—"that Molly Graham and the harbor grant."

Molly had a different subject on her mind.

"I'm still thinking about the murdered man, Michael."

"Yesterday Paddington told us it could take quite some time to learn his identity. They'll have to use dental records."

"I was thinking about talking to some of the people who live near the cliffs."

Michael nodded. "I agree completely. Another mystery to solve." He winked. "I'm sure Paddington will be delighted."

"I'll bet he already has someone on it."

"If he can spare anyone," Michael reminded her. "I'll bet every constable is scheduled at the marina today."

"I'm sure he'll focus on nothing but the murder tomorrow."

They didn't say anything for a few moments, just locked eyes. "But you want to do some investigating of our own," Michael offered.

"It'll keep my mind off this fiasco," Molly admitted, nodding toward the front window. "Actually, I've been thinking about that chewing tobacco tin."

"Ah…the little green tin Paddington pulled out of the corpse's pocket. Maybe find out who sells that brand around here?"

"And if any young men regularly buy it. That would narrow the possibilities."

She noticed people glancing her way, some hiding

their faces behind steaming mugs of tea or the lami-
nated menus. For a moment she considered getting up
and leaving, but things hadn't wholly calmed down
outside—she could still see the constables and planning board members hustling through the crowds. The
beautiful Draghici girl strolled by the window, two
teenage boys dutifully following her. A cameraman
walked past, getting color shots. Molly desperately
wanted to avoid the media for at least a few blessed
minutes, even though earlier this morning she'd been
looking forward to doing a few interviews.

"Be careful what you wish for," she muttered.

It was her turn to hide behind the menu she hadn't
relinquished to the waitress when she caught sight of
a reporter in one of the booths. An old-style recorder
was on the table, and he sat, leaning forward on his
elbows, chatting with Clement Horsey, owner of a shop
selling dockside bumpers, ladders and the like.

Michael followed her gaze. "Old Clement was
against it, right?"

She nodded.

"You'd think the reporters would talk to someone
in favor of the project. There's loads more of them."

"But they're probably not as interesting." Molly
shushed him with a finger to her lips. "I want to hear
what Clement is saying."

She knew Horsey had celebrated the "double nickel"
this year, but to her he easily looked at least a decade
older than fifty-five. Exposure to salt air and sun had

weathered his skin to the point that it resembled aged, cracked leather. Even his eyes seemed old, a rheumy blue. She liked him, but she wasn't sure she was going to like what he was saying to the reporter.

"The whole town hasn't gone aggro over this," Horsey said. "There's only a few of us opposed to all the work." He ran his fingers through the few strands of hair on the top of his head.

The reporter waited for him to continue.

"I'm not saying fixing the harbor is a bad idea. It's not. In the long run it's ace, I suppose." Molly couldn't make out what Horsey said next, because the waitress returned and clunked their glasses of pineapple juice in front of her and Michael.

Molly picked up the conversation again and strained to hear over the background noise.

"...just that some on the planning board are playing favorites."

The reporter leaned farther forward, as interested as Molly in this angle. "Can you elaborate, Mr. Horsey?"

"S'pose it's just my personal opinion, but I think the whole thing's a bit dodgy. See, two of the planning board members own businesses on the wharfs. They're gonna get some of that grant money, and I believe they're going to get more than their fair share. It's not all been set who's getting what, you know. They're still working that out. But why wouldn't them two take as much as they need for themselves?"

"And you'll be left out?" the reporter asked.

"Well, not entirely. Already got some funds marked for me. But not enough to cover everything to bring the place up to the new codes, and I doubt any more money will come my way. I'm gonna have to dig deep into my own pocket. Barnaby—the bloke who started all the ruckus this morning—it's gonna cost him the most. His place is falling apart, and the town's forcing him to do the fixes."

"Forcing?"

Horsey's nod was so exaggerated he reminded Molly of a bobblehead doll. "They'll not renew his licenses, the Blackpool council, until he does. They're putting teeth into their plan to clean up the area. They've passed tougher building codes, and they'll close him down if his place doesn't meet them. He's got reason to be right pissed and I don't think he'll belt up about it. They should leave 'im alone, you know. Let Barnaby keep his licenses without doing any of the work, let the building fall down around him, and then sweep away the pieces. Wouldn't take much more than a strong wind to flatten the dump."

Horsey drained the contents of his cup in one long swallow and thunked it on the table to get the attention of one of the waitresses.

Molly's frustration grew with every word. "Michael, he's off-base. There is plenty of grant money to go around. I told him that we're still waiting to hear on a couple more applications I have out there. And if this first grant won't cover enough, I'll find another one to apply for. No one should go belly-up over this. Barnaby, Horsey—they're just worried and reactionary. They're..."

At that moment their waitress returned, setting down a bowl of yogurt in front of Molly that would have cost a pittance in a grocer's compared to the price on the menu. Michael dug into his omelet and would have replied but Molly shushed him as she heard Horsey continue.

"I've butted heads with the planning board," Horsey said once his cup was refilled. He had raised his voice and was attracting the attention of most of the café patrons now. "Said my piece to Molly Graham, but she's not the one giving away the grant money. That's all the planning board. Said my piece to the board, too. Nothing's gonna come of it. I still have to make the changes the plans require, and the grant money's not gonna cover it all. Like I said, you should talk to Barnaby. He'd give you some real colorful quotes for your article. You could maybe even print some of them."

The reporter chuckled, stopped his recorder and turned the tape over, restarting it.

Molly finished her yogurt and stared into the bottom of the plastic cup, her desire to march over there and set the record straight warring with her growing sense of despair about the whole thing.

"You really did do a good thing, getting the grant."

Michael ran his index finger over the back of her hand, raising goose bumps. "Horsey's right. Barnaby's Bait Shop is a ruin, a real eyesore that might not be worth fixing. The sea, the salt and the wind in the fall, especially…they all take a toll on the buildings. And the businesses aren't going to repair themselves."

Molly ran her thumb around the top of the cup. "Yeah, I know it's a good thing, Michael. I just wish someone else had gone after that grant."

"Not another soul in town has your expertise." He shoveled in the last mouthful of eggs and speared a piece of banger, holding it up and waving it like a conductor's baton. "Some of these folks couldn't organize a piss-up in a brewery. Mark my words, sweetheart, when this is done, they'll all be singing your praises." He popped the sausage in his mouth and swigged down the last of his pineapple juice, then nodded to the clock on the wall. "Got about five minutes before the official ceremony."

Molly pushed back from the table. Her hand lingered on Michael's. "Join me?"

"Wouldn't miss it, love." He scanned the bill and left money on the table. "After you, Mrs. Graham."

Not more than a dozen steps beyond the café's front door, Molly spotted Jennessee again. She was now interviewing Edwin Barker, the owner of the narrowest building along the wharf, where he sold boating supplies such as cushions and oars, and an assortment of T-shirts the tourists favored.

"It's all impractical," Barker said into the microphone in front of him. "I sell to independent fishermen, mostly, and making these renovations won't help my sales. The fishermen don't care what my place looks like…but they will after I have to raise my prices to help cover the expense."

"So you're not getting enough of the grant money." Jennessee didn't pose it as a question.

The color was bright in Barker's cheeks. "No way, I'll have to pay so much out of my own coffer that it'll put me out of business. But maybe that's what the planning board wanted all along. Put me and Barnaby out, buy up our places cheap and turn a good profit for themselves. That's what they're planning, I'll wager. That's it, I say."

Barker worked at something in his mouth, chewing gum or tobacco. "You can ask them, but they'll come across all selfless, saying this is for the good of Blackpool." He spat a blob on the ground, and immediately Molly thought about the murdered young man with the tin of chewing tobacco. "They can go to hell as far as I'm concerned. They're all a bunch of arses and—"

Molly gritted her teeth. She suspected—hoped—the interview would be edited before it was played on the news tonight. At least things seemed to have settled down for the most part. No one was fighting, the reporters were either interviewing townspeople and board members or staking out a place behind the ribbon for the ceremony. She counted five constables in addition to D.C.I. Paddington, and they were all keeping a wary eye on the crowd.

"My children will inherit nothing but loads of debt. Oh, and a historical building with a mortgage they can't afford—"

The rest of Barker's tirade was cut off by a dissonant screech, feedback from the microphone on the podium. Planning board chairman Arliss Hogan was adjusting it so it didn't tower over her.

"Let the real show begin," Michael said. He stepped away from her and walked over to Barker for a moment.

"Some show," Molly muttered, wondering what Michael wanted with Barker. "Let it all be over with soon."

"After this chaos, I'll happily go back to my mummies on meteors," Michael said, returning. He patted the pocket that contained the iPhone and grinned at Molly. "After, of course, we visit the shop where Barker buys his chewing tobacco. There's only one tobacconist in Blackpool, according to him."

"Good work," Molly said.

Dennis Carteret climbed up the stairs to stand behind Arliss. Percy Lethbridge, in front of the gathering, spotted Molly and waved, then headed her way, sidestepping Aleister Crowe, who was talking to another reporter.

"Today begins an important chapter for Blackpool," Arliss began. For such a petite woman, she had a loud, deep voice, and Molly thought she could get along without the microphone. A few people from the town council joined her behind the podium, and Molly wondered if the wood platform would hold them all. "Today we kick off improvements to our storied wharf that will preserve our town's history for the coming generations."

Polite applause followed more of her practiced words, and then Arliss stepped back and Carteret took a turn.

"You were all witness to an unfortunate incident a short while ago, when our friend Barnaby Stone—"

"Put on quite a display, he did!" someone in the front hollered. The remark was followed by a round of chuckles.

"Much thought was put into this project," Carteret continued, raising his voice. "I'm not just a planning board member. I'm one of those businessmen who own property on the wharf. I, too, will be spending some of my own money. In the end, we'll have buildings that meet Blackpool's new codes and will stand against time and the sea. This work will prevent our precious buildings from deteriorating and will preserve our town's past. If we lose our history, we lose part of ourselves, who we are and who we were—good people and notorious scoundrels, heroes and villains, colorful souls all. But more than that, we would lose our heritage."

The applause was loud and Molly released the

breath she'd been holding. Maybe this would be a good day, after all. Everyone but the Draghicis and the few opposing business owners were clapping and cheering.

Lethbridge finally found his way to her. "It's a good speech," he pronounced. "Heard him practice it a few days ago."

"What did you want to talk to me about earlier? Something to do with the marina?"

He hesitated. "It can wait," he said. "Let's listen to him."

Carteret went on about Blackpool being blessed with the grant money Molly had obtained, and mentioned which buildings would be renovated first and the order that the others would follow. He gestured behind him to the water, and described the dredging that had started several days ago and would ultimately deepen the channel. Although he spoke clearly and the microphone carried his voice to the very back of the audience, he was suddenly drowned out by a chorus of voices approaching from the street.

"Say no! Say go!" It was a chant that crashed like a tall wave over Molly. "Say no! Say go!"

She spun around to see a gaggle of T-shirted young men and women, all carrying signs with slogans:

Dredging is Dreadful
They're Dredging our Graves
Go Green Gladiators
Stop the Digging!

Keep the Water Safe
Dredgers are Murderers
Fish Slayers!
Green Gladiators=Blackpool Heroes
"Say no! Say go!"

So much for ending the day on a positive note. She turned to Michael, frustrated. "Let's get out of here."

CHAPTER FIVE

"MAYBE WE CAN ACTUALLY accomplish something good today," Molly told Michael. "Why don't we visit that tobacco shop." She wasn't one to shrink from conflict, but she knew that arguing with protestors or TV reporters wouldn't do her or the renovations any good. If anything, her presence might fuel the naysayers.

"Sure, we'll walk over to the tobacconist, look around—"

"Ask a few questions—" Already Molly was brightening at the thought of doing a little sleuthing to take her mind off the protest at the marina.

"—see what we can find out."

"Then we'll drop you at home to your waiting undead, while I come back and face this…"

Garrison Headly shot past them, microphone out, attempting to be the first reporter to interview the protestors. Jennessee Stanwood was fast behind him, with their respective cameramen following.

The air was instantly filled with the murmurs of the townsfolk and tourists. Someone shouted "Bring back Barnaby," and the constables blew their whistles.

"What a nightmare," someone grumbled near Molly. "This has become a real dog's dinner."

Michael and Molly turned to go, but Garrison Headly was directly in Molly's path. Michael tried to steer around him, but the protestors pressed in from the street side, and the crowd surged forward from the dock side. Molly and Michael were caught between the two groups and had to inch their way through.

Headly managed to pose for the camera. "This is Garrison Headly with BBC Four, reporting from historic Blackpool, where a ceremony just got underway…and has been interrupted…by a group of environmentalists apparently calling themselves the Green Gladiators. I'm speaking with their leader, Francis Weymouth."

Molly stopped in her tracks, belatedly realizing the man beside Headly wasn't just a part of the crowd. The color drained from her face.

"The day can't get any worse now," Michael said flatly.

"We've tried to reason with the planning board— and with Molly Graham," Weymouth said, eyes straight at the camera.

"We've been against the changes to the docks from the very beginning, and we've been consistently ignored."

Weymouth had outdone himself today, looking trim and reasonably professional with pressed pants and a sport jacket over a bright Green Gladiators T-shirt. In his early thirties, he could pass for someone a decade younger, with sandy hair and intense blue eyes. Molly had to admit he was striking to look at, with his broad shoulders and square jaw, and he was perfect eye candy for the news cameras.

But just because he was attractive didn't mean she liked him. In fact, he set her teeth on edge. She didn't trust him, not since she'd first seen him at one of the planning board meetings. She'd learned then that he lived in a shack at the edge of town, calling himself "off the grid," because he had no need to rely on electricity or other modern conveniences that "stressed the environment." Though apparently he had no qualms about the convenience of using his motorcycle to get around. He hadn't been arrested yet for any of his numerous and noisy demonstrations regarding the harbor project, but he had been charged for trespassing on construction sites and damaging equipment to "preserve the balance" of the land.

Molly didn't doubt that he was an environmentalist, but she suspected he relished the publicity more than any actual change he might accomplish.

"Short-term, dredging will hurt fishing in the area," Weymouth explained. "Long-term, it will have a dire impact on the lobster population and lobster harvesting. It's a lose-lose situation," he added. "Nothing good will come of—"

"There was an environmental assessment done," Molly countered loudly, drawing the reporters' attention. Jennessee—appearing out of nowhere—and Headly quickly thrust microphones in front of her, as Michael stepped behind. "Mr. Weymouth's concerns were all addressed in the multiple assessments we commissioned. Yes, dredging will have a big impact on the ecosystem of Blackpool's harbor, that's why it wasn't entered into lightly. But the impact will be favorable."

"How so?" Headly and Jennessee said practically in unison.

Molly pulled in a breath. "A deeper harbor can accommodate larger boats, which is beneficial for our fishing and tourism industries. Plus, the silt that has accumulated on the ocean floor carries traces of contaminants like PCBs and heavy metals that are harmful to aquatic life. Ridding the harbor of them will be a boon to the ecosystem and healthier for the residents of the town. We wouldn't have been awarded such a large green grant if the project caused harm."

"Liar!" a protester shouted.

"They can make their bloody studies say whatever they bloody well want!" chimed in another.

"Bring back Barnaby!" someone behind her called. She thought it might have been Barker.

One of the Green Gladiators waved his sign, bopping it on the head of a tourist, and the crowd began to turn ugly again.

Molly heard D.C.I. Paddington shout for order, then Michael called to her. The reporters dove into the mass of people with glee as Molly headed toward her husband's voice.

"You can't do any more here," Michael said. His fingers closed around her elbow, and he gently led her through the mob of shoving, arguing people.

They emerged on the street behind a group of the red-hatted ladies, who had also had enough.

"Looks like Weymouth is backing off," Michael observed as he glanced over his shoulder.

"He got what he came for," Molly said.

They crossed the narrow street and walked toward downtown.

"You're right, you know," Molly added. "I couldn't have done or said anything to make matters better back there. I'm not on the planning board."

"Thank God for that."

"I have no real power over any of it."

He pulled her into a long hug. "But you have power over me."

"You're sweet," she said.

"You really did do a very good thing, Molly dear, getting that green grant."

"Tell me that again and again," she said. "And maybe tomorrow I'll start to believe it."

"Cheer up, we've still got a murder to solve."

It was black humor, but strangely it *did* lift her spirits. "Right—the tobacco shop. Let's go."

CHAPTER SIX

THE TINY STORE WAS CALLED Havana Haven, and it was marked by a carved wooden Indian standing outside the door, hand raised to its brow in a salute. The statue was nearly life-sized, and Molly was surprised she'd never noticed it before...not that she'd ever had an occasion to visit a shop like this.

Still, it was a pretty storefront—red wooden trim against a dark green front, brick accents, narrow windows flanking the door. On display in the window were pipes and pipe stands, cigar boxes, a sun-faded smoking jacket and all manner of accoutrements, such as cigar cutters.

Inside, it smelled like tobacco, naturally, though no one could smoke inside. She and Michael were the only customers. The odor was neither bad nor pleasant, but it was strong. Molly took a quick glance around.

A glass-fronted counter showed a variety of forms and types of tobacco, and the shelf behind it held pipes, lighters, pipe cleaners, tampers, ashtrays and the like. On the opposite wall were humidors, cigars, matches in colorful containers, Native American figurines, replicas of Blackpool's lighthouse, jigsaw puzzles, T-shirts, hip flasks and a stand with magazines and postcards. In short, the place was packed with stuff.

A woman strolled in from the back room and stood behind the counter.

"Can I help you?"

Molly hadn't thought she'd come here with a preconceived notion of who would be minding the store, but she wasn't prepared for the proprietor. The woman was a little younger than Molly, trim and well-dressed.

Michael held out his hand and the woman took it. "Michael Graham," he said by way of introduction. "And this is my wife—"

"Molly," the woman finished. "I've seen your picture in the paper. From America."

"New York," Molly said.

"I'm from Boston." She paused a moment. "Sandra Kettle, of the Boston Kettles. And a graduate of the Pennsylvania Tobacconist College."

"You have a degree in…tobacco?" Molly didn't bother to hide her surprise.

"Yes, graduated two years ago. My parents wanted me to be a dentist. Instead, I'm a certified tobacconist." She pointed to a framed certificate on the wall behind her. "I know how to treat for beetle infestations, how to grow and harvest, how to set up a humidor, the best way to evenly light the foot of a cigar and how to store them."

"Fascinating. However did you come to Blackpool?" Michael asked.

"Met a fellow at the college. He was from Blackpool, so I followed him here. He returned to the States to pick up another degree, and I decided to stay." She smiled broadly. "Places around here aren't as anti-smoking as in America, so it's a better fit."

"We're not here to shop," Molly said. And for no particular reason, she added, "We don't smoke."

"Figurines? Puzzles? Got a new shipment of both." Sandra indicated a stand in the corner. "Magazines?"

"Actually, we're here about tobacco," Molly said.

"Chewing tobacco," Michael elaborated.

Sandra pulled a face. "I sell it, but I don't recommend it. Mouth cancer and all that. Not as much risk with a pipe or a cigar. Still, some folks seem to enjoy a good chaw." Like a TV hostess showing off the prizes available on a game show, she pivoted and pointed to a smaller counter toward the front filled with tins and packets. "Name your poison."

"You're not the only place in Blackpool selling chewing tobacco, are you?" Molly asked.

Sandra seemed offended. "I'm the only tobacco shop, but the little convenience stores sell it, too, though their prices are higher."

Michael and Molly stepped over to the counter. Michael turned to squarely face Sandra. "We're looking into a murder," he explained.

"And you think my chewing tobacco killed someone!" Sandra sounded appalled.

Michael shook his head and offered a friendly smile. "No, not at all. It's just that the dead man had a tin of chewing tobacco in his pocket."

"We figured if we found out where he bought it," Molly explained, "we might find out his name."

"Aren't the Blackpool police looking into this… murder?"

Molly nodded. "But I found the body."

"And so you're helping?" Sandra immediately wanted to know all the details, and Molly supplied what she could while she looked over the wares, searching for a tin that resembled what they'd seen.

Sandra had a large variety—Big Mountain, Cannonball Plug, Chattanooga Chew, Cotton Boll, Apple Jack, Bowie, Days O' Work, Durango, Oliver Twist, Red Man, Southern Pride, Morgans, Mail Pouch, Lancaster, Work Horse, Stokers, Starr—but none that were familiar.

"I don't see it," Molly said.

Sandra appeared crestfallen. "Well, can you describe the tin?"

"I didn't get close but it was green, right Molly?"

"Yes," she agreed, "and it had eyes on it."

"Blue eyes?"

Molly straightened. "Yes! Green can, blue eyes. I think it might have been a wolf."

Sandra shook her head. "No, that would be a husky. The chewing tobacco brand is Husky, and if it was a green can, it was either wintergreen long or wintergreen fine."

"And you don't carry it," Molly said flatly.

Sandra looked smug. "No. It's a relatively common brand, and I tend to cater to folks with more discernible tastes."

"Oh, well, thank you—" Molly turned to leave.

"But I do special order Husky wintergreen fine for a young man here in town. It's the only brand he chews." Sandra headed toward her cash register, opened the drawer, and pulled out a small notebook. "My customer's name is Clark Partridge. He says Husky tastes awesome."

"Do you have an address for him?" Molly was eager.

"No. No address. But I have a phone number." Sandra jotted it on the back of her business card and passed it over.

"It's a mobile number." Michael fished for his cell phone and gave it to her. She dialed the number, barely breathing, but it just kept ringing. "No answer. Doesn't go to voice mail."

"Should've mentioned that," Sandra said. "You either get him or you don't. He told me he didn't know how to set up the voice mail on his mobile."

"Or he might not be picking up again ever," Michael said. "Clark Partridge might be dead."

CHAPTER SEVEN

PADDINGTON REGARDED THEM coolly, as if they were children who had interrupted a very busy parent rather than the ones helping him solve his case. "Clark Partridge, huh? Thought I'd seen him before, but I couldn't be sure at the time with the decomposition and damage from the fall."

"Clark Partridge," Molly repeated, annoyed that they had rushed to the D.C.I. excited to crack open the case only to be swatted down. "We probably can't be sure until the coroner's report, right?"

Paddington nodded. "If there are any dental records. The young man you found had horrible teeth. Probably hadn't been to a dentist in the past ten years."

"But you know—knew—this Clark Partridge?" Michael asked. "Were familiar with him?"

"A grufty tough if ever there was one," Paddington said, relaxing a little. "A real ne'er-do-well. I arrested him for flashing 'bout a year ago, shoplifting a few months before that. Partridge, a worthless git if ever there was one. Graduated to worse crimes maybe, or fell afoul of someone he rubbed the wrong way and who decided to rub him out."

"So he was a local?" Michael asked.

"We haven't confirmed that this *was* Clark Partridge," Paddington warned, "but it seems likely. The coroner guesses he was murdered only a day or two before you happened across the body, Molly."

Molly shuddered. "You'll tell us if it really is Clark Partridge?"

Paddington stood, hesitating. "I truly appreciate your interest…though you should leave this kind of work to me and my department. We're able investigators, and we would've found our way to Havana Haven after the big marina show shut down. I've only got so many officers, you know."

Molly studied the tips of her shoes, reproached. "But if it is Clark Partridge—"

"Yes, yes it will go a long way toward finding out who killed him, Molly." Paddington escorted them out the door. "Now, why don't you busy yourself with the planning board and the marina, and leave the detective work to me?"

MOLLY SAT ON THE window seat in her office, looking out over a flower garden in bloom. The late morning sun made the water in the birdbath sparkle like scattered diamonds. The window was open a crack, and she drew the scent of the outdoors deep into her lungs, the roses and fresh-mown grass pleasantly mingling with the hint of leather from the old books on a nearby shelf.

She really did love this place—this old house, Thorne-Shower Manor, the town, the climate. Despite the ruckus at the harbor two days past, she considered herself terribly lucky to be in this lovely English coastal town.

She'd grown up in crowded, loud Queens, New York, and in only five years managed to gain a double master's in business and communications from NYU. It had been hard work, and she'd sacrificed anything resembling free time to do it, but it was worth it. As a result, she became a sought-after professional grant writer for a few New York City businesses and nonprofit organizations with fees that amazingly put enough money in her bank account so she'd never have to work another day in her life if she didn't want to…and she was only thirty-two. In the course of all that, she'd met and married Michael, and moved to Blackpool with him. At first they'd intended to make Thorne-Shower a holiday home, but quickly decided they wanted long-term. Michael was successful, too. His computer games were best sellers, making him wealthy in his own right.

Money would never be a problem.

So she could have put her feet up this year rather than pursue the big green grant for Blackpool's harbor. But Molly was never one to sit on the sidelines, and the notion of retirement—at any age—didn't sit well with her.

She shuddered and drew her knees up, wrapping her

arms around her legs. Had she embraced the wrong project this go-round with the harbor? She couldn't get the image of Barnaby being hauled off by a constable out of her head, or the leering face of Weymouth with his Green Gladiators sign waving back and forth like the stick on a metronome.

We Give a Damn, his sign had read.

Well, she gave a damn, too, which was why she'd gotten involved.

Yes, he'd argued against the plan during the first meeting she attended. There had been other opposing voices at most of the meetings. Some of the older townsfolk objected to any changes that would increase tourism around the harbor. These were "hardliners" who considered the tourist trade evil and something to avoid rather than promote. They maintained that Blackpool should be only for residents, and that locals needed no more than the land and the sea, not the presence of visitors. Of course, those comments had stuck in Molly's craw, and were met with looks of disdain from the townspeople who ran antique shops, bed-and-breakfasts and chartered fishing trips.

More reasonable were the concerns of Barnaby and his ilk, but they hadn't been very vocal in the planning board meetings, and Weymouth and his fellow Green Gladiators had provided a quiet opposition at that time. The presence of all those cameras and reporters had apparently incited them. Or had they been that determined all along? Had she been so excited by the prospect of all the renovations that she hadn't listened?

But even if she had, would she have done anything differently? In her heart she knew this project was the right thing to do. She recalled words from Carteret's speech: "This work will prevent our precious buildings from deteriorating and will preserve our town's past. If we lose our history, we lose part of ourselves."

As for those worried about the cost, Molly had applied for additional historical preservation grants from private corporations, and if they came through it would mean even more funds that would lessen the financial burden. That would end Barnaby's objections, Clement's, too. If they had to pay next to nothing out of their own pockets, she knew they'd embrace the project. But more money wasn't a sure bet.

In the meantime, her life had been turned upside down. She'd been hefted up on a pedestal by the planning board and town council, been praised publicly by most of the businessmen…but damned by Barnaby and a few others. And the Green Gladiators? They'd probably love to skewer her with the stakes on their protest signs.

She'd never intended to spend so much time and energy on the project, never imagined it would consume her like this. But she'd thought of nothing else since the clash at the groundbreaking ceremony. The past couple of nights she'd tossed and turned, dreaming about Barnaby calling for her to be drawn and quartered out on the docks.

Her stomach was constantly in knots, and she wondered if she might have an ulcer. She was drowning in worry and the stress was affecting her health.

She'd be falling to pieces soon if she couldn't find a way to deal with it.

At least the ruckus had died down in the last couple of days. Dredging continued. Renovation was proceeding on the dock businesses. From what she'd heard, only local reporters had ventured out on the wharf since the ceremony had turned into a melee. Of course, plenty of reporters—local and otherwise—had been calling her to continue their coverage long-distance.

Somehow Paddington had kept the murder quiet. She hadn't read a single word about the dead man on the cliffs. It seemed all the newshounds were so caught up in the marina, it hadn't been noticed.

She'd been relying on the answering machine to keep the reporters at bay…along with the Green Gladiators, who were proving to be a nuisance. And the Grahams' housekeeper, Iris, screened the calls she picked up.

A few reporters had somehow gotten a hold of Molly's precious new iPhone number—she'd managed to replace the one she'd lost over the cliff. She'd been letting those go to voice mail but she checked it periodically to see who she really needed to call back.

Percy Lethbridge was the one person who had not phoned. He had wanted to talk to her about something at the groundbreaking, and it was disturbing her a little that he hadn't followed up. She supposed if it was important, he would find a way to reach her, but she had a sense something was off.

Think about Clark Partridge instead, Molly told herself, and who might have killed him. They still didn't have confirmation on the body's identity, but Molly just knew it was Partridge. The Husky wintergreen can seemed confirmation enough.

"Molly?" Iris poked her head in the doorway. She held a portable phone. "I think you should take this call." Her hand was over the receiver end, but she was talking loud enough that whoever was on the other end would realize that Molly was home.

Molly eased off the bench and met the housekeeper in the middle of the room.

"It's that Arliss Hogan woman," Iris continued. She passed Molly the phone. "It's about a boat."

"A ship," Arliss corrected when Molly said hello. "It's a ship, not a boat, and a big one from what I gather." The planning board chairman's normally deep voice was an octave higher in her excitement.

"What ship, Arliss?"

"That engineering company, the one dredging the harbor—their men have discovered a sunken ship!"

Molly sucked in a breath.

"Isn't that amazing?" Arliss continued. "I've called

the board members. It's too bad all those reporters from London and Manchester are gone."

"Too bad," Molly mused.

"But not to worry. I have their business cards. I'll call them back and—"

"Wait, Arliss!" Molly spoke louder than she'd intended. She forced herself to adopt a calmer tone. "There's been enough news coverage of the harbor. Besides, the media will hear about the ship soon enough. I'll be right down."

"Well, at least that darling Jennessee Stan—"

"Why don't we wait until we have more information about the ship?"

"Well, I suppose—"

"I'll be right down," Molly repeated.

She hung up and handed the phone back to Iris.

"About lunch…"

"I'll get something in town," Molly said.

Molly hadn't taken but a few steps out of the room when the telephone started ringing again.

She went upstairs and stuck her head into Michael's office. "There's a sunken ship in the harbor," she announced.

Michael and his friend Rohan were seated at a large table, intent on a project in front of them. Neither appeared to have heard her.

"I'm going downtown," she said.

First stop the marina, second…a return to Havana Haven. Molly had thought of a few more questions to ask the certified tobacconist.

CHAPTER EIGHT

THE PHONE RANG THREE TIMES before it was picked up.

"I think your Mrs. Dunstead deserves a bonus, mon," Rohan said.

"She ought to let them go through to voice mail and help us sort through them later," Michael replied.

"Now that wouldn't be so interesting, eh? Mrs. Dunstead would be missing out on the chance to tell those blooming reporters where to go."

Rohan Wallace was even more of a newcomer to Blackpool than Michael and Molly. A chance meeting on the outskirts of town led to Michael and the Jamaican becoming fast friends, and they often found a reason to get together. Usually, however, they met at local pubs, and alcohol was almost always a component. Tea filled their big mugs today, however.

The phone rang again. Four times this go-round.

Michael knew Molly had stopped answering the phone after the commotion at the docks. She looked at any receiver as if it were a hungry cobra waiting to strike her.

He had been tempted to pick up the phone himself,

but he suspected the calls were about the renovation project—either reporters, planning board members or, God forbid, the big Green Gladiator himself, Francis Weymouth. If any client was calling about Dead Space or Michael's previously released games, his mobile would have been chirping. Paddington knew that number, too, but Michael doubted the D.C.I. would have an identification on the dead man yet. DNA tests took a long while.

Another series of rings.

"Someone won't give up." Michael made a move toward the phone on his desk, then stopped himself and returned to the table.

"This is my only day off, mon," Rohan continued. "I don't want to spend it worrying about a telephone. Just unplug it—we need to get going on this."

"Only day off? Are you working six days a week now?"

A nod. Rohan had been hired to do some of the upgrades around the harbor.

"Up from four when they hired you?"

"Boss put me up to six yesterday. Bumped my whole crew up. I think all the noise at the harbor is making him want to hurry up the renovations. All fruits ripe with me. I can use the money." He flexed his considerably muscled arm. "And the exercise."

"That's a job you might not have—"

"If your Molly hadn't gotten that government money. I know. The crew I'm on—we're going to rip out one of the walls in a tavern tomorrow, and the front siding. The wood's just rotten." He shuddered and made a face as if he'd bitten into a lemon. "It's all the sea air; the salt eats at the wood. Tough work, but I'm up for it." He flexed his other arm. "And the money's good—but not as good as the payout if we're lucky with this, mon. I'll have as much money as you, and I'll never have to lift another hammer again if I don't want to. I'll never be a *quashi,* a peasant, anymore. I'll be a rich, rich mon."

Michael laughed good-naturedly then scowled when the phone rang again. Five times and it went to voice mail.

"Iris is letting the machine take them all now," Michael mused. "She might be missing out on some juicy gossip."

"Don't worry about the phone, mon. Better to spend your time on this." Rohan pointed to the maps spread out on the table in front of them. "Your Mrs. Dunstead will start answering the phone again after she finishes fixing lunch."

"Which she's making special for you."

"Aye, mon. Ackee and saltfish. You'll like it."

Michael's office was normally a spacious room, but it felt cramped because of the table they'd moved in to hold the architectural model of Blackpool that he and Rohan were constructing.

His office was on the third floor and already crowded with a draftsman's desk, three desktop computers, a fresh-out-of-the-box notebook computer, a net book and a big, polished walnut box for his iPhone that was fully loaded with different software applications to interface with Bluetooth devices and infrared. A smattering of action figures perched on the shelves between graphic novels, comics and a collection of history and New Age books.

The desk had been pushed toward the wall to accommodate the big table they'd just brought in along with extra chairs—comfortable high-backed ones with deep, leather-covered cushions. They'd been outside in the hall, where no one sat, and Michael had decided to put them to use.

There were other rooms he and Rohan could have worked in, but this office was his domain, and Molly usually stayed out. She considered it a mess, which it often was, and respected his "sanctum." More likely, he thought, she just didn't want to see all his clutter. He wasn't as respectful when it came to staying out of her office, but she never seemed to mind his intrusions.

Michael had actually wanted to spend the day with Molly asking around about Clark Partridge—help keep her mind off the harbor woes. But Rohan had been insistent about working on the models.

"Does Molly think you're toiling away on the vampires on Mars?"

"Probably. She isn't crazy about my fascination with the treasure, so I find it's best not to mention this project."

Just saying the word *treasure* sent tingles running down his skin. It was why the Draghici family was in town. It was why a few reporters were hanging around with the excuse of covering the harbor renovation. And it was why Rohan was spending his day off here.

Rumor persisted that Charles Crowe, Blackpool's founder and the architect of many town buildings, had buried gold and other treasures somewhere in Blackpool. For the past century and a half the townsfolk had searched for it…and a few had been killed over it. Some claimed there was a curse attached to the gold— put on it by the Gypsies it was stolen from—and that was why it had remained buried; the elder Crowe had feared to spend the money or give his family access to it. Despite the time that had passed the Gypsies currently in town still considered the gold their property, adamant that Crowe had robbed their ancestors. Stefan Draghici had sworn a blood oath that he would get their gold back.

Local historians debunked the notion of Gypsy claims and curses, however, believing that the mysterious fortune once belonged to a rich duchy from Eastern Europe and that the elder Crowe had bested the royals in a business deal to gain it. Aleister Crowe—current heir to Charles's legacy and fortune—much preferred this version.

Either way, whoever found the treasure could make a solid, legal claim to it.

All sides suspected the cache would be worth millions in the current market.

Not that Michael needed the money. But the treasure hunt was a real-life game that beat any glitzy computer program he could devise.

And Rohan could certainly benefit from it.

Rohan stabbed a finger at a diagram of an old Victorian house that had been converted into an art gallery and boutique. Next to it were ultrathin pieces of plywood, of the variety used to construct model aircraft.

"So we're going to build the town out of these little hunks of wood?" He shook his head, beaded dreadlocks clacking.

"Yes. I've already made a couple. These blueprints are copies of Charles Crowe's originals. I want to make a set of architectural models like the library has. Though certainly not as fancy."

"Why, mon? Why don't we just go to the library and look at the one there?" After a moment Rohan brightened, the smile reaching his eyes. "Ah! All fruits ripe, mon. If we build our own model, no one will know we're looking for the treasure. And no one will pick up any clues from us."

"Exactly," Michael agreed. "We're not sharing what we find with anyone else. I'm hoping that since Charles Crowe designed many of the town's buildings, recreating them will reveal hints of where his secret tunnels are…and his treasure. Besides, the library isn't open late enough at night to use their model."

Michael set out the few buildings he'd made and reached for a piece of wood. It had pencil marks on it, and he started cutting the next section of walls. The wood was thin enough that a big pair of scissors worked well.

Iris tapped on the door a few minutes later, and Rohan opened it with a bow and a flourish.

"Ackee and saltfish, gentlemen," she announced. She set the tray on a corner of the table, covering up part of one map. "The ackee is canned, Rohan. Sorry. Coffey's Grocery had to special-order it. Probably couldn't get it fresh." She scrunched her face up as she studied the food.

"Ackee is African," Rohan explained to Michael.

Michael thought it looked like overly large berries.

"Ackee trees were brought to Jamaica in the seventeen hundreds. The fruit's delicious." He paused. "But poisonous if you eat it before it's ripe. The fish…?"

"Cod," Iris supplied.

"Perfect," Rohan said, taking one of her hands in his and kissing the back of it.

"You make me blush, Rohan." She stepped away from the table, shaking her head.

Rohan leaned over the tray and inhaled. "Mmmm. Reminds me of home."

"Blackpool's your home now," Michael said.

"Aye, mon. At least for a while. But once we find this gold, I can buy an entire city in Jamaica and have you and Molly over for *fresh* ackee."

Iris made a tsk-tsking sound. "You're like children, you two. Swotting over all those drawings on your ludicrous treasure hunt."

"You think Michael's obsessed with the treasure, Mrs. Dunstead?"

"I think *both* of you are obsessed," she teased. She turned on her heel and left the room, closing the door behind her. "A waste of time, Molly would say!"

Rohan raised an eyebrow. "Why doesn't Molly approve of our treasure hunt?"

Michael shrugged. "She doesn't believe the gold exists."

"You love your Molly, right?"

"More than life itself, my friend."

"How'd you two meet?"

"I donated to some children's charities she'd been writing grants for."

"In the United States?"

"London, actually. She was there promoting a kids' education project tied to one of her grants. It was one of my favorite charities at the time." He laughed. "She thought I was a berk at first, I'm sure of it. But I was persistent. I didn't give up—asked her out over and over until she finally said yes. I'd look her up when I went to the States, and she'd find me when she was over here. It was fate, I believe, the two of us getting together. I finally proposed and asked her to move to England. She said yes, and now we're here."

"So Molly believes in you, but not the treasure?"

"That's it in a nutshell. She dismissed it as some local legend that's grown out of proportion through the decades. She says I'm being silly."

Rohan imitated the housekeeper's tsk-tsking sound. "You know what I think?" He didn't wait for a reply. "I think she's hoping you and I find it. And now we'd better eat this lunch before it gets cold."

Michael watched Rohan dig in to the meal, but only picked at it himself. He didn't mind the ackee, but he never much cared for cod. So he ate just enough to be polite. Besides, his mind was churning over the maps and diagrams. He just had a sense that these models held the key to finding the treasure….

"Old man Crowe, he didn't know architecture," Rohan observed as he put together the crookedly designed Good Scents shop. Michael, watching him work, thought that while Blackpool's original contractors might not have understood the principles of building, Rohan certainly did. The Jamaican's miniatures put Michael's to shame.

"Nevertheless," Michael said, "Crowe designed most of the oldest buildings. Some of them have tunnels underneath them, and secret rooms. The odd shapes? Not all of them are off-kilter, though the customs house has a crooked backside."

"Aye, to hold cursed treasure, right, mon?"

Rohan reached for the marker to draw in another window.

"That's the idea."

They continued uninterrupted for a while until Iris came in with more tea and removed the lunch tray.

"I'm making a streusel cake for dinner," she stated.

"Yum," Rohan said.

"I was planning for around six," she said.

"Sounds fine," Michael confirmed.

"Or should I hold dinner in case Molly isn't back yet?"

"Back?" Michael straightened.

"She told you she was going out," Rohan said. "Downtown."

"She did?"

"You weren't paying attention, mon."

"Did Paddington ring her?" Michael asked. "Did he identify the body?"

"What body?" This from Rohan.

Michael waved his friend's question away.

"No, Arliss called her," Iris said. "Not about a body. About a sunken ship. And you'd know all about it if you listened to your wife."

Michael spun and went to his desk, pulled out his mobile and punched the button for Molly's new iPhone.

"A sunken ship, huh?" Michael asked when she

picked up. "Down in the harbor?" He paused and listened to his wife. "A big one?"

Rohan raised an eyebrow. "Don't plan on me for dinner, Mrs. Dunstead. I've a mind to take in some of that salty sea air."

CHAPTER NINE

DRIVING IN HER Mini Cooper, Molly's route had taken her down Dockside Avenue and past the Havers Customs House. Alfie Lochridge was outside the nearby Mariner's Museum. He was the museum's director and local expert on the maritime and pirate histories of Blackpool. His long gray hair was in a ponytail today. He was wearing his customary suit and bow tie, and she slowed to wave at him. She liked Alfie, even though he sometimes butted heads with the Historical Preservation Society and the planning board. Still, he'd championed the wharf renovation project and had helped Molly gather some of the data for her grant proposal. She figured Arliss would call him about the ship soon, setting notions of pirates dancing in his head.

She loved looking at everything when she drove, never tiring of a single building or feature. A perpetual tourist, Molly sometimes thought of herself, admiring the dwellings, taverns and shops that butted right up against the sea and stretched out along the wharves. Historically, the town had grown up embracing the sea trade. Now it embraced tourism.

The architecture throughout the area was varied.

Victorians sat next to sprawling manses with Gothic overtones and Tudor buildings that could grace the covers of magazines. There were even clapboard wood-and-brick dwellings that had stayed in the same families for generations.

But today she didn't allow herself time to enjoy the town; she'd do that on the ride home. Molly sped up and passed the Blackpool Café, Coffey's Grocery—above which nested the Other Syde Haunted Tours with its odd brother-sister proprietors who read fortunes to supplement the tours—and Coffey's Garage. The last could use more than a little renovation, she thought, housed in a weather-beaten sheet metal building that had seen better days.

Molly passed the Old Town Hall, one of her favorite buildings. It was one of the simplest places Charles Crowe had designed, and the years and weather hadn't marred its charm.

She slowed when she went by Havana Haven; she would stop there after she met with Arliss. Next, she caught sight of the lighthouse, seemingly too squat to function effectively. It still operated, but primarily as a gift shop and scenic lookout, where for a few pounds visitors could enjoy an excellent view of the harbor. In Blackpool's early days, brigands used to douse the light in the tower and set fires along the coast to lure in unsuspecting cargo ships. The ships would break apart in the shoals, and the brigands would go out in small boats to salvage the valuables.

Molly had read all about the town's "mean years," as Alfie called them. During the mid-1700s a royal ship that belonged to King George III fell victim to the trap. The king had family on the ship, and they all drowned. Subsequently soldiers came searching for the brigands, catching and executing as many as they could find.

Town officials wouldn't let the lighthouse go dark after that. On All Hallows' Eve the lens was traditionally changed to red, to symbolize the blood that was spilled at sea and to keep the spirits of the shipwreck victims at bay.

Maybe Arliss's sunken ship dated back to that time. Molly shuddered at the notion that the ship and its crew had been lured onto the shoals.

An odd stroke of luck let her find a close parking place at the marina, and she eased the Mini in before anyone else grabbed the spot. There was very little parking around Blackpool proper, and Molly was used to walking blocks upon blocks to get anywhere.

The sounds and smells today were more agreeable than those that had assaulted her the morning of the groundbreaking ceremony. The marina was always noisy, but in a good way. There was the almost-musical "clink" and "thunk" of lines striking masts, boats bumping against docks, bells, tugboat bleats and the ever-present cry of the myriad beggar gulls. The marina was home to hundreds of vessels, a mix of fishing boats and pleasure crafts—all the colors on an artist's pallet spread out across the water.

She admired the view for a few minutes, the snow-white sails against the dark blue sea, the smattering of reds, greens and yellows from pennants and painted hulls. She scanned the natural breakwater that was about two hundred yards out from the shore, a sandbar that protected the harbor. The dredging crew was on the close side of it.

There was a gathering on the largest dock, and Molly spotted Arliss in a flowery red-and-peach dress, the skirt billowing around her knees in the slight breeze. Taking a deep breath of the salt-and-fish-laced air, she headed in her direction.

"Wonderful," Molly grumbled, her good mood deflating at the sight of Jennessee Stanwood. The reporter and her cameraman were among the group on the dock, as well as one of the writers for the local paper. At least it looked as if the rest of the media circus had packed up and left town, and hopefully Arliss could be persuaded not to call the newshounds back.

"Molly!" Arliss waved a white-gloved hand. "Over here, Molly! Yooooo-hoooooooo!"

I see you. And where else would I be going? Molly thought, irritably. But she put on a cheery face and walked a little faster.

Percy Lethbridge and Dennis Carteret were there, along with a few other planning board members and a constable. Percy was rocking back and forth on his feet, like a bored schoolboy waiting to be dismissed.

Aubrey Crowe was also in the mix. A 22-year-old version of Aleister, Aubrey was no doubt serving as his older brother's eyes and ears. Molly disliked him only a little less than Aleister, finding him more cordial and not quite as manipulative. Stefan Draghici was at the end of the dock, looking out over the water but probably keeping within earshot of the assemblage.

As she sidestepped Jennessee, Molly was pleased to note the reporter didn't have a microphone and that her cameraman was taking color shots of the boats sailing out past the sandbar.

But the woman seemed to be in a chatty mood. "Good thing we decided to stay in Blackpool," Jennessee said, falling in step at Molly's side. "The other media left, though Garrison Headly with BBC Four is downtown doing a special on the Romanian gold and the gypsies that are here to claim the treasure. Do you think the ship is connected to the treasure?"

Molly opened her mouth to say something, but Jennessee kept going.

"I booked rooms for me and Jordan—he's my cameraman—at this little bed-and-breakfast. Brilliant! Thought we might get a lot more on the harbor story. I was right."

"Brilliant," Molly echoed. A few more steps and she was part of the group.

"Molly, Molly, Molly," Arliss tittered. "It's because of you the ship was found."

"I hardly think—"

"If you hadn't gotten us the grant, we couldn't have hired the dredgers, and they wouldn't have dug in to the silt." Arliss gestured wildly, her gloved hand looking like a bird she was trying to shake away. "Things happen for a reason, I always say. You're part of all this, so that's why I called you, dear."

Molly gritted her teeth. She enjoyed the endearment when Michael said it. But it felt wrong, almost patronizing, when it came from Arliss's too-red lips. *Dear,* indeed.

"I wanted you to come down here and get the news firsthand."

"Thank you." Molly didn't know quite what else to say.

"And I did just as you asked," Arliss continued. "I didn't ring the media. But I didn't have to. Miss Stanwood was already at the docks, and our local man—"

Molly let the rest of Arliss's words drift over her until Arliss turned to introduce a man at the dock.

"Molly, this is Mr. Quentin Jones," Arliss began, "of—"

"QJ Dredging," Jones interjected. He shook Molly's hand. It was a firm grip and his fingers were calloused, the skin brown like the bark of an oak.

"Molly—Molly Graham—acquired the grant that funded the dredging that revealed the ship."

"The find is a good one, actually," Jones remarked. "A large ship, reasonably intact. It was under a thick blanket of silt, and doing anything with that ship will postpone most of the dredging. I'm not willing to risk any lawsuits." He had a rough-sounding voice, as if he had to push the words from his throat, but Molly liked the sound of it. It reminded her of recordings of old New Orleans blues singers.

"I've called a good friend of mine, Algernon Hume-Thorson, and he's agreed to come out first thing tomorrow and take a look. Algernon is a professor, and one of the best underwater archaeologists I know. He's advised on a few of my other contracts when we've unearthed some unexpected ships. Likely he'll talk me into halting all the dredging work. We'll see what he has to say."

Out of the corner of her eye, Molly spotted Stefan edging closer, not hiding his interest in their conversation. She ground the ball of her foot against the wood. The dock wasn't private property; Stefan was free to stroll it.

"Can't tell you how old it is yet," Jones continued. "But my guess is a hundred years or so. One of those tall ships."

Jennessee and her cameraman had found a position off to one side, where they could record Jones without anyone blocking their shot.

"D.C.I. Paddington says he'll post constables on the dock twenty-four seven," Arliss said. "Just like you asked, Mr. Jones."

"Well, that's up to Blackpool, not me," he said. "But it's a precaution I recommend to keep people from diving on her and looting…provided there's anything there worth stealing. She might have already been cleaned out." He took a deep breath and rolled his shoulders; it was a tired gesture, and Molly wondered how long he'd been out there working today. "But better to err on the side of caution, as they say."

Jennessee thrust her microphone at him. "When will you know more about the kind of ship and—"

"After Professor Algernon takes a look." Jones nodded to her, and then to Arliss.

"Now, if you don't mind," Jones concluded, "I want to get back to my crew while we still have daylight hours."

Not waiting for a reply, he turned on his booted feet and went back down the ladder to his boat.

Arliss and the others resumed chatting, Jennessee interjecting questions, and the cameraman switching angles from the group on the dock to the men in the boat and the dredging crew.

Molly quietly extricated herself and slipped away from the dock. The mobile in her pocket started playing a classical music piece and she reached for it. "Michael?" She paused and listened. "Yes, there's a sunken ship. Apparently it's a big one, maybe a hundred years old or so—"

"Molly?" It was Lethbridge. She swung around and gave him a weak smile. "I mentioned a few days ago that we needed to talk."

She told Michael she'd call him back later.

"Yes, you did, Percy. I got a little distracted." *With a dead body.* "All the newsmen and Barnaby and—"

"I got distracted, too. Busy few days, yes." He cupped her elbow and politely steered her toward her car. "But we can talk now, right?"

"Yes, certainly. What is it you—"

"It's about the grant money."

They'd reached the car and a silence settled between them. Molly waited for Percy to go on. She thought she'd covered all the aspects of the grant at the various meetings they'd had. The grant money was in the planning board's hands, and she really had nothing more to do with it.

"Yes?" she finally prompted.

"Some of it is missing."

Molly felt her heart rise into her throat.

"Eighty-five thousand pounds, maybe more. Could be as much as a hundred. A lot of artful accounting was done. I'm surprised I noticed it, really."

"You have to be wrong. Tell me that—"

"No. I'm not wrong." He started rocking back and forth again and wrung his hands nervously. "No, no. I'm not wrong."

"Don't say anything." The words came out in a rush. "Not a thing. Not to Arliss. Not to the town council. Certainly not to a reporter. Not yet. Not until a proper accounting can be done. Let's be sure the money is gone before we raise any red flags."

He swallowed hard and craned his neck toward a line of boats moored in the harbor. "Best raise your red flag high, I would think. And make it a very big, bright one."

CHAPTER TEN

MOLLY LEANED AGAINST the side of her Mini Cooper. The metal had absorbed the warmth of the afternoon sun, and it was pleasantly toasting her backside. She hardly appreciated the sensation, however. She felt as if she'd been punched in the gut.

It had taken her endless hours to wade through the paperwork to apply for the grant and now to learn that some of that money was…what was the word Percy had used? *Missing.* How could you simply "miss" that much money?

"Actually, I wasn't the one to find the discrepancy," Percy said, interrupting her thoughts. "Arliss was going over the books a handful of days ago, the day after the groundbreaking ceremony, it was, and saw something that didn't add up. She's no financial whiz, that Arliss Hogan, but she's nosy, and her eyes fell on an item." He took a deep breath and plowed on. "She's been into every aspect of this project, like a nanny directing school children. She said she wasn't going to 'carry the can' for the board on this, even though she's at the top. She called Henry—"

Henry Cuthbert…another planning board member,

Molly thought. Henry worked for one of the banks in town and had supplied her with some of the figures she'd used on the grant applications.

Molly felt numb. "Who was doing the books? Who's responsibility is this?"

"Responsibility?"

"Yes, who on the planning board was keeping track of the money? I only got you the grant. Your board was supposed to watch the funds, allocate who got what. I thought no money could be spent without at least two signatures. When did—"

"After Arliss settled down, I looked at the figures again and saw what she was upset about. One row of numbers didn't add up, though it was hard to spot. Lord knows how she noticed it. Anyway, I was supposed to give Henry a turn at the books this morning—I'd been storing them at my place. But then this whole shipwreck thing came up and—"

"So you had the books."

"Well…yes." Percy rambled on for quite a while, saying the same thing really. Molly kicked herself for not listening to him the day of the groundbreaking ceremony.

Molly was surprised Arliss hadn't called her about the discrepancy. "What did you say to Arliss to calm her down?"

"I told her it must be a simple mistake that can be set right, that she didn't need to broadcast anything until—"

"So Arliss is waiting until Henry examines the records before she goes public with this?"

"Right. The shipwreck has given her something else to think about…at least for the moment."

Molly sighed as she saw Aleister Crowe pull up in his Bentley. Aleister created his own parking space, easing his big car into an area designated for loading and unloading sailboats. Percy stopped midsentence and watched Aleister get out of the car, silver-topped walking cane gripped in his right hand.

He headed straight toward them, a tight smile painted on his face. It was meant to look friendly, Molly was sure, but to her it was surreal, reminding her of the expression on a department store mannequin.

He tipped his hat, his widow's peak glistening as if he'd slicked it back with mousse. "Mrs. Graham. I was hoping to find you here."

She nodded and thrust her hands in her pockets, intending to avoid any offer of a handshake.

"You heard about the shipwreck, Aleister?" This from Percy.

"Yes, yes. My brother Aubrey happened to be at the marina when word of it broke a little while ago. Good thing Aubrey just happened to be around, eh?"

Just happened to be around, Molly thought. *There was always a Crowe somewhere convenient…or inconvenient, depending on your perspective.*

"And you thought you'd come down to have a look," Percy said.

"Quite." Aleister rapped the bottom of his cane against the ground. "And I'm quite pleased to see you here, Mrs. Graham."

Molly forced herself to offer a weak smile in return.

"I never got a chance to compliment you on what has come to pass so far with the harbor project." He paused, as if waiting for her to say something. When she didn't, he continued. "You are aware that I was in favor of the refurbishment from the beginning. Though I suppose I could have made my support more formally known."

You supported some of it. But you didn't want your buildings along the wharf touched. Somehow you managed to keep a select few out of the proposal. What don't you want the construction workers to find, Aleister? What skeletons do you have in your closets?

At least he'd never publicly opposed the proposal during any of the meetings. That was something, she realized.

He paused when a small tour bus pulled up and a gaggle of elderly people got off, more red-hatted ladies in the mix.

"But I can tell you now that I was one of those anonymous donors that helped pay for the environmental impact study. And I will continue to champion the board's efforts. Perhaps I *will* be a little more public about it." He pointed his cane at Arliss and her gathering on the dock, then, as if he was sighting down the barrel of a rifle, he moved the tip of the cane to point at the dredging platform. "I'll stay on the scene, Mrs. Graham, to offer my moral support, throw a little more money the harbor's way if necessary. Now, if you'll excuse me, I've a mind to chat with Aubrey."

He tipped his hat again and left the pair.

Molly relaxed a little. There was something about Aleister that didn't sit well with her, like a burr that had found its way inside one of her fancy open-toed sandals.

Molly felt her stomach twist and again worried that she might have an ulcer. Barnaby's outburst at the groundbreaking, the long hours of work she'd put into the grant, the possibility of money missing, the murder of the young man on the cliff trail. Her head was throbbing, the pounding so loud it all but blotted out the sound of the water lapping against the pilings.

"So that's what you were trying to say to me the other day before Dennis's speech, that some of the grant money had gone missing?" Molly asked, resuming her conversation with Percy. "You should have told me then. Not put it off and—" She frowned. "Wait a moment. You said Arliss found the problem *after* the ceremony."

"Yes, well…"

"So what did you want to tell me then?" Molly felt her stomach twist even tighter in grim anticipation.

Something worse was coming, wasn't it? "What did you not say the day of the groundbreaking?"

"Actually, that is what I wanted to talk about that day—the grant money."

Percy stepped in front of her, blocking her view of the gathering on the dock. But out of the corner of her eye she saw more people approaching from the street and cutting through the marina's tiny parking lot. A few board members, Garrison Headly of BBC Four and his cameraman, some of the downtown business owners, a few regulars Molly often saw in the Blackpool Café, Alfie Lochridge from the Mariner's Museum, some folks she didn't recognize—maybe tourists. Word about the shipwreck had spread quickly. Alfie walked faster than usual, an excited spring in his step. Molly suspected he was…what was the phrase Michael used…chuffed to bits about the news of a shipwreck.

Some people were leading off the dock, too—Dennis Carteret and a reporter for the local paper. They were headed toward Percy and her. Thankfully, Molly realized Jennessee and her cameraman stayed on the dock.

D.C.I. Paddington pulled into the last tiny parking lot, blocking Aleister's Bentley. Shoulders squared and chin thrust out, he made straight for Arliss and her group.

"Yes, well…" Percy's jaw twitched. "I did want to mention the missing grant money to you the day of the groundbreaking ceremony. I almost called you the night before about it."

"So you knew before Arliss?"

He scowled. "Yes."

"Who took the money?"

"Me," he answered. "Well, not me alone. I just helped actually."

"You? You helped—"

"And doctored the books. But not well enough, apparently. Arliss saw—"

The knot in Molly's stomach twisted so tight that she could hardly breathe. The pounding in her head was deafening.

"*You* took the grant money."

"Yes, well…but not all of it. And I didn't do it alone."

"Who was in it with you?"

"Dennis. He needed the money. I just double-signed for it. All checks from the fund require two signatures, and—"

Molly's mouth had gone desert-dry.

"You and Dennis Carteret stole—"

Carteret reached her a few steps ahead of the local reporter. He opened his mouth to say something, but the reporter rushed in, flipping open a notebook and meeting Molly's gaze.

"Mrs. Graham, I've caught word that some of the grant money for the harbor restoration project is

missing. Arliss Hogan mentioned a problem with
the accounting. Do you care to comment on that?
Mrs. Graham…"

CHAPTER ELEVEN

MOLLY SAW D.C.I. Maurice Paddington pacing before the gathering on Blackpool's largest dock and saw her chance to escape the reporter and ask about the dead man. Paddington had two constables with him, and they were keeping an eye on the growing throng drawn here by news of the sunken ship.

"Excuse me, I think the D.C.I. is waving to me." She hurried away from Headly and Lethbridge—though she'd have to find a way to get back to Percy and Dennis.

She was relieved when she got to the D.C.I. Paddington had told Molly on more than one occasion that he'd envisioned his final few years as head of the Blackpool Police Department to be relatively quiet ones. She knew he'd had enough excitement in the early years of his career. Over coffee one night he'd recounted tales from the days when he worked a beat in London. He'd dealt with more than a few murders, particularly in the less savory parts of the city. He'd even worked on a serial killer case, though it was never solved. Blackpool had seemed like a peaceful town, and Molly suspected that was why he'd sought to work the last years of his career here.

But the murder of Clark Partridge, the missing grant money, the commotion the harbor renovation had caused…and now the sunken ship had hijacked any plans for a quiet ending to Paddington's career— not to mention all the other events that had stirred up the town since the Grahams had moved here.

Some Blackpoolers jokingly called the detective chief inspector "Adolf Brown," a mash of Charlie Brown and Adolf Hitler because of his large round head, small mustache and military walking style. He commanded the respect of the townsfolk, but whether that was because of his bearing or D.C.I. title wasn't clear.

Before Molly could speak to Paddington, Sergeant Luann Krebs came out onto the dock, the heels of her shoes making a snapping sound against the wood. Krebs likely had her sights set on the D.C.I.'s job when he retired. She relished taking charge of any challenging situation.

Paddington barked a few orders to Krebs to oversee the marina.

He respected Krebs, Molly deduced, but it was clear from his mannerisms that he didn't much like her.

Krebs stopped in front of Paddington in a parade-rest pose. Molly stood several feet back. "D.C.I. Paddington."

"Sergeant."

"I know I'm early, but—"

"That's fine. I've always prided myself on punctuality."

"The Green Gladiators have gathered downtown," she reported.

"Lovely. Are they causing trouble, Sergeant Krebs?"

"No, sir. But if I know Weymouth and his cronies, I expect they'll be marching down here...where the people are. Bring more attention to their cause."

"Any signs?"

"They're carrying a few, but not like the other day."

"Well, that's something, I suppose." He looked beyond her and noticed Molly. "Mrs. Graham...if you've a moment?"

"Actually, I want to talk to you, too," Molly said.

"Try not to arrest anyone today, Sergeant Krebs."

"I'll do my best, D.C.I."

"Oh, D.C.I. Paddington!" It was Arliss, and her tone stopped him before he could turn to Molly. "A word with you."

"Certainly." Paddington stroked his chin while he leaned near the woman, who spoke too softly for Molly to eavesdrop on the conversation.

The D.C.I. nodded, gave a mock salute to Krebs and finally stepped toward Molly.

"I feel old today," he told her. "Like a man at the end of his nineties." His steps across the wood planks toward the shore were heavy, almost plodding, as he kept up with Molly. He stepped around a patch of fresh gull droppings and politely nodded to Alfie, who was mumbling excitedly about the sunken ship.

"You must be stressed," Molly observed.

"Yes, I am that." Paddington shook his head. "I'm not the town's manager, and yet I feel like it, trying to juggle the council, planning board, my own department, the Green Gladiators, the historical society—" he took a deep breath, which sounded like dry leaves shushing across a stretch of pavement "—and the various clusters of business owners who are alternately happy and venomous about the renovation project. Throw the media into the mix…not that I need to complain to you about that. The station's phones are ringing with journalists wanting reports of any further altercations since I had Barnaby carted away. I released the old cuss the next day, you know, slapping him with a small fine and a warning not to cause trouble again."

"The media can be difficult," Molly admitted.

They'd reached the end of the dock, and she noticed Lethbridge and Carteret were gone. The local reporter had moved on to speak to someone else, but there was a piece of paper on her windshield.

"Just two more years," he said.

"Is that all?" Molly asked.

"Two more years and I'll retire," he said. "Just two more years."

"Blackpool will miss you."

He made a huffing sound. "Not everyone, I'm sure. Now, I have my men keeping tabs on a few disgruntled shop owners, particularly Barnaby, and Clement Horsey, whom I consider the ringleader of the opposition. I doubt any of these suspects will carry through with their threats, but I have to be careful."

"So you're stretched."

Another huffing sound. "Spending the money on overtime because of the marina, assigning someone to follow the Draghicis, keeping an eye on my strained budget. And to top it off there's the murder."

"Do you have a positive identification?" Molly asked.

"Pretty sure it's Clark Partridge. That's what I wanted to tell you. DNA evidence isn't back yet. Can't find any dental records on him. But no one's seen Partridge for days, none of his usual mates. Got some partial fingerprints, and we're running them now. We don't have the fancy system they show on television programs, but I'm hoping for something tomorrow. Wish the prints had been better. But the birds and the crabs and such…you know. Anyway the build matches, as does Partridge's love of Husky wintergreen."

Molly made a face.

"But I don't want you getting involved in that. What's this about missing money?"

"She told you about that."

He nodded, his fleshy jowls jiggling. "Talked about

it a moment ago, all quiet like. Not that such a bulldog of a woman can keep anything secret."

"About that grant money—"

"I told her I'd look into it. If there's a problem with the harbor fund, it could be bad all the way around for Blackpool. I pray this is all one of those proverbial wild-goose chases, and that Arliss hasn't read the books right."

He spun around when a series of whistles cut through the air. The crowd was growing larger on the main dock, and the inspector shielded his eyes against the sun to make out what was going on.

A scuffle, it appeared, with Sergeant Krebs trying to take control of the situation. And the Green Gladiators were arriving, just as Krebs predicted. How could the dock hold so many people?

"Don't go anywhere," Paddington told Molly.

Bracing himself with a breath of sea air, Paddington retraced his steps to the dock, pulled out his whistle and blew it as he went.

"Say no! Say go!" Francis Weymouth hollered. He led the Green Gladiators and was dressed more like a tourist today than the natty impression he presented during the groundbreaking.

"Say no! Say go!" the men and women behind him chanted.

People crowded around the end of the main dock, while others edged out onto smaller ones. Still more spilled over the wharf area. Marina business owners poked their heads out of their establishments, tourists jockeyed for a good position. Digital cameras came out to capture the action.

Molly saw someone fall from the dock into the water.

"The blighter shoved Brent!" a man hollered.

Krebs blew her whistle again.

Clement Horsey was in the mix, Barnaby close behind him.

"I need reinforcements," Paddington yelled into his mobile. "Of course at the marina. Where else do you think?"

CHAPTER TWELVE

MOLLY READ THE NOTE on her windshield and reached into her pocket for her mobile. "Michael? Meet me at the Blackpool Café. Try to hurry." She hung up with him and dialed Percy Lethbridge and Dennis Carteret.

Twenty minutes later she and Michael were in a booth, seated across from the two planning board members.

"I can't believe you left the marina without talking to the D.C.I.," Molly said to the two men. "He was right there. You could have come clean about the…theft."

Michael had already been brought up-to-date on the missing grant money.

"Yes, yes, of course we have to speak with Paddington," Percy said. "Just not yet."

"Honestly, we'll tell the D.C.I.," Dennis added. "But we wanted to speak to you first."

"All right—talk, and quickly," she told them. She reached for a menu, her fingers wanting to fuss with something.

Michael scanned the menu she held. "A piece of

peach pie and a large milk," he said to the waitress, who had stepped up to the table.

"Nothing for me," Molly said. "I don't have an appetite."

"Coffee," Percy said. "Black."

"Bring the pot," Dennis added, "and those pink packets of sweetener."

"So what's going on?" Molly urged. She'd lowered her voice to a conspiratorial whisper, even though there weren't many diners in the café.

The men waited until the coffee arrived and Michael speared into his piece of pie.

"We took the money," Dennis began.

"*You* took the money," Percy corrected.

"*You* helped. It was for me, but it wasn't just me. You helped."

"Did I have a choice?"

"Fine." Michael glowered at them. "We've established that you're thieves. That you've ruined some of the hard work Molly did by getting the grant. And, lord knows, you've ruined your reputations." He finished his pie in a few bites and pushed the empty plate aside.

"So Molly and I are here," he continued, "and we're listening. But I think the D.C.I. should be hearing your confession, not us. And I think you should be in jail."

Dennis tapped his thumbs against the tabletop. "We'll talk to Paddington soon, promise. I don't see as we have any choice. We've…*I've* made a real dog's dinner out of this, and I'll pay the piper when the time comes."

Molly traced a whorl in the tabletop with her thumb. "Why did you take the money?" She spoke softly, the words forced. The men's revelation had been a blow to her. Michael was right, she'd put a lot of effort into getting the grant, and now to have some of it stolen… and worse, by people she'd trusted. "You're both successful. The grant is covering most of the work slated for your building, Dennis. You certainly have enough to pick up the rest of the tab. I don't see why—"

"My daughter has been kidnapped," Dennis blurted. He instantly lowered his voice when he saw a table of older women staring at them. "My daughter has been kidnapped and the only way I could raise enough money for the ransom was to steal from the harbor fund."

The color had drained from Dennis's face, and he tapped his fingers faster, his breath ragged. Before Molly could ask the particulars, he started crying.

"Rosamund, my daughter, is everything to me, you have to understand."

"Kidnapped?" Molly's throat tightened.

"I got a call a few days before the groundbreaking. The caller said he had Rosamund. And he wanted a lot of money."

Molly leaned closer. Dennis's voice had dropped so

low she had trouble hearing him. "Why didn't you go to D.C.I. Paddington? Why didn't—"

"The man said no police. Rosamund's my only child." Tears welled at the corners of Dennis's eyes. "She's my precious, precious child. I'd do anything for her. He said if I called even one constable Rosamund would die."

"See? We couldn't tell the D.C.I. and risk something happening to Rosamund," Percy added.

Michael let out the breath he'd been holding. "So you took the grant money to pay the ransom."

"What choice did we have?" This from Percy.

"Lord knows she's been away enough already." Dennis's shoulders shook. "I sent her to the very best schools…got her away from here in her middle years. I spared no expense. She had so much trouble, my Rosamund. Her mother died when she was a child. And now…maybe she's gone for good."

Michael stretched out a hand and grasped Dennis's wrist. "So the kidnapper hasn't released her?"

He shook his head. Thick tears were falling down his cheeks. "I sent her to boarding school to keep her away from some of the low-life young men around here—and now some damnable lowlife has her. Good God, that kidnapper has ripped out my very heart."

"You paid the money," Michael said, "and you don't have Rosamund back yet?"

Dennis seemed to shrink. "No. Not yet."

"You have to tell the D.C.I." Molly's voice trembled. "You have to tell him everything."

Dennis shook his head more vehemently. "The kidnapper said no police. I can't risk it. Maybe…maybe he'll still let her go. He's had the money for days now. My Rosamund…"

Molly knew who Rosamund was, though she had never spoken with her for any length of time. The girl was twenty-two, beautiful, though she hid her figure in baggy clothes.

Percy held up his hand when the waitress approached, his stare enough to turn her away.

"You see, Molly, Michael, we didn't have any choice but to take the money from the fund to pay the ransom," Percy said. "You understand, don't you? It was the only way we could get that much money fast enough."

"He demanded a hundred and fifty thousand pounds," Dennis said. "Immediately. I couldn't get that much so quickly…not on my own. I managed to liquidate some stocks and such, withdrew my savings, sold a few bonds. I came up with sixty-four thousand in a matter of hours. But I couldn't manage any more."

"The rest we borrowed from the harbor fund. Eighty-six thousand," Percy said.

"I could have sold my house, my marina business, some other things," Dennis offered. "But none of that would have been done soon enough to meet the kidnapper's demand. I couldn't let Rosamund die, you understand. My heart. Rosamund's my heart."

A bell rang above the door, and they looked up to see an elderly couple enter. They took seats at a table by the front window.

"Rosamund—" Molly began.

"We dropped the money where he told us to, but no word from the kidnapper since," Dennis said. "Nothing. But I won't bring the D.C.I. into this. I won't. The kidnapper has my mobile number." Dennis touched his pocket. "And he said he'd call when she was safe. But he insisted—"

"—no police," Percy finished. "We only came to you because Arliss stuck her nose in. Word about the missing grant money is going to get out now."

Michael cleared his throat and let go of Dennis's wrist. "Which is all the more reason that you have to tell the D.C.I."

Dennis slumped back into the booth. Tears continued to pour down his face. "He said he'd kill her if I went to the police." A silence settled between them, then he added, "But what if he's already done that? What if he picked up the money and killed her anyway?"

Molly tried to drag the man's thoughts away from that possibility. "How exactly did you get the money from the harbor fund?"

Percy sighed. "We wrote the check so Dennis could cash it, but I entered it in the books as a payment to a construction company, like it was all aboveboard. We'd cut a similar check the previous week for the same company. And that's what Arliss noticed, the second check. She's usually so scatty. How could she have spotted that the company was being paid twice, different amounts, for the same work? At least she didn't cobble on to the fact that Dennis and I took it." He scowled. "But she is pointing a finger in my direction."

"I intended to return the money," Dennis said. "I was going to sell something, my house, business, holdings—whatever, to make up that money. And I'll still do that, I say. I've got time now. Time while I wait to hear about Rosamund. Dear God, don't let her be dead…."

CHAPTER THIRTEEN

"SHE'S MY LIFE, you know, my only child," Dennis repeated. "She's all I have. I tried to call Rosamund right away, thinking this must be some horribly bad dream, and that she was all right and enjoying her holiday—and that no one had her. That the kidnapping was some sick joke."

Percy shook his head. "But Dennis couldn't reach her. Not on her mobile. Not at the hotel where she was supposedly staying. Not at any hotel we called. We tried some of her friends—nothing. So we took the money. We managed to get to the bank just as it was closing for the day and cashed the check." He grabbed his coffee cup. He held it so tightly his knuckles turned white. "Then we dropped it off at dawn, right where we'd been told."

"And we waited," Dennis said.

"And nothing yet," Michael said.

"I finally went to the groundbreaking ceremony the day after—didn't want anyone to know something was amiss. Didn't want to give the kidnapper any reason to hurt my little girl. I gave my speech as planned."

"No one called during the ceremony," Percy said.

"So we waited."

Dennis shook his head, his jowls hanging down. He had the look of an utterly defeated man. "And nothing has happened. I am ruined. My daughter is still gone. I stole money from the harbor like a common cutpurse. I broke the law. And I have no idea what's happened to my daughter."

They sat in silence for several moments, listening to the click of the waitresses' heels against the tile floor. Their own server set the tally on the table and took away Michael's empty plate.

"More milk?"

"Yes, please," Michael answered.

"More coffee?"

Dennis and Percy shook their heads, and she walked away.

"Do you have any idea who could have taken Rosamund?" Michael raised the question, but Molly had been thinking it.

"No." Dennis rubbed at his chin. "I've asked myself the same thing, over and over. Had to be someone she was friendly with, though. Someone who knew she was out of town on a holiday."

"We've been trying to sort through it all," Percy said. "That day at the groundbreaking...I wanted to tell you about it then, Molly."

"Did you mention to anyone that Rosamund was away?" Molly asked.

"A couple members of the board," Dennis answered.

"I probably brought it up in conversation. I don't have Arliss's gift of gab, but I say too much. I told some of the men who own businesses near mine at the marina. I'm always talking about my Rosamund. And the people who work at my restaurant."

"Barnaby?" Molly wondered aloud. "Did you tell Barnaby?"

"I suppose. Maybe Clement, too."

Percy nodded. "You know Barnaby and Clement never wanted the renovations we forced on them with all our new codes and such. Do you suppose one of them could have kidnapped Rosamund for spite?"

"No." Dennis slapped his hand on the table. "Barnaby certainly could use the money. He's a dill when it comes to saving. Squanders everything on beer, I think. But he'd never do something as complicated as kidnapping. It would be too much work."

"Then maybe someone else at the marina did it, someone who actually supports the project but doesn't like you, Dennis." Percy shrugged, the gesture wrinkling the fabric of his jacket. "Maybe someone who wants to see Dennis ruined."

The other man brushed at his face. "Percy and me, we've been through this 'til we don't have the energy to talk. Can't think of anyone who'd want to hurt Rosamund. Can't think of anyone who'd be so…evil."

"Why ask for one hundred and fifty thousand pounds?" Michael mused. "Why not two hundred thousand? Or an even hundred?"

"I suppose anyone at the marina could have set it up," Percy said. "Money is an issue with all of them right now. The green grant isn't covering everything."

"And much less now," Dennis said. "But I *will* pay the money back."

Molly stared past the two men and out the front window. A few people strolled by, one with a Green Gladiators sign over her shoulder.

Francis Weymouth. Could Weymouth have been so fired up about stopping the dredging that he engineered the kidnapping? He was smart, Molly was well aware, and as relentless as the sea itself. He might have reasoned that Dennis Carteret didn't have the funds to meet the ransom demands. And he knew the man would have had access to the harbor grant money. Would Weymouth have stooped to such means to siphon off the funds and block the project?

Who else wanted the project to stall?

Could the Gypsies have stumbled upon this as a way to get money to bankroll their members until the so-called treasure was found? Would Stefan Draghici have known who was in charge of the harbor funds and how to target with a kidnapping plot?

"I understand why you didn't go to the D.C.I. before," Michael said. "Maybe I wouldn't have done anything differently. But I think you're wrong not to go to him now. Let the police look for the kidnapper."

Dennis shook his head again. "The kidnapper said no police. We dropped off the money—"

"Where?" Molly asked.

Dennis squared his shoulders. "Right where the kidnapper told me. On a narrow trail above Jack Hawkins's nose."

"Hawkins's nose," Michael whispered. He nudged Molly's leg under the table.

"Dennis," Molly said, "the D.C.I. is going to be coming to you anyway. Arliss already mentioned the discrepancy with the grant fund."

"The woman's nutters sometimes," Percy grumbled. "Can't keep her mouth from flapping. She'll say I had the books and was writing the checks, that I—"

The bell at the restaurant's door rang and D.C.I. Paddington and Sergeant Krebs walked in. Seeing the Grahams and the two board members, they made their way over.

"About the missing grant money," Paddington began abruptly. "I've been looking into this and—"

Dennis stood up. "I did it," he said. "I stole the grant money. It was all me."

Percy scooted out of the booth and stared down at the tips of his polished leather shoes. "But I helped him."

"I hope you two know good barristers," Paddington said. "I have to arrest you."

Molly thought Sergeant Krebs seemed overly happy to slap the cuffs on the men. It was the first time she'd seen the female constable genuinely smile.

"I had good cause," Dennis said.

Paddington held up a hand. "Tell me all about it at the station."

They left quickly, the other diners staring open-mouthed.

"I guess they stuck you with the bill," the waitress said as she cleaned off the rest of the dishes. "You can pay at the counter."

Michael left an overly generous tip on the table.

Molly and Michael made it halfway to the door before Alice Coffey—the head of the Historical Society—intercepted them. A towering stork of a woman, she gazed at them with her beady gray eyes. The spinster had caked on her makeup today, making her face look like pale tree bark dusted with chalk, and her lips were accented by a sparkly pink lipstick, a shade favored by teenagers.

"Molly Graham."

"Good day to you, Miss Coffey." Molly tried to sound pleasant. She didn't dislike the woman, but had never warmed to her. Rumor was that she'd killed her betrothed five decades ago after learning he'd cheated on her.

"I've been talking to Aleister," Miss Coffey said, waving her hand and sending a cloud of her too-sweet, too-strong perfume Molly's way.

"About the renovation, no doubt."

"Yes. Yes. He's concerned about one of his buildings down there."

"He only *has* one building to be renovated, Miss

Coffey. He managed to keep the other three off the list."

"Well about this one, I think he's right, it should be excluded as well."

"It's not really his building. If I recall, it's in Aubrey's name."

"Still. It isn't in quite such bad shape as the others, you know." She leaned in close, giving Molly another good whiff of the perfume. "I think he just doesn't want the contractors poking around inside, you know. Can't say as I blame him. There might be secret rooms or passages, things he hasn't discovered yet and doesn't want some thug with a hammer to destroy."

"Miss Coffey, the Crowes have to meet the same building codes as everyone else. And I—"

"They give so much to Blackpool, Mrs. Graham."

"And I did not set the updated codes. All of that was done by the planning board. I'm not on the board, and I didn't influence the members. All I did was go after the grant money for them."

Coffey made a huffing sound and clicked her teeth together. Molly thought they were too perfect and too bright to be real.

"Yes, Yes, Molly. But if you hadn't gotten that grant, the renovation would have been put off for years."

"So you're against the work being done? But at the last meeting—"

"Young woman, I'm not against the work at all."

"But you—"

"I just think you ought to find a way to take that Crowe building off the list for renovations. Be a good dear and see what you can do."

CHAPTER FOURTEEN

MOLLY AND MICHAEL headed out the Blackpool Café's front door.

"Don't you dare take Aubrey's—or Aleister's—building off the list," Michael said. "Let Spinster Coffey plead her case to the planning board."

They hadn't taken more than a dozen steps before they spotted Jennessee Stanwood jogging toward them, microphone out, cameraman in tow.

A local reporter was behind her. Edward something, Molly remembered. She spun around to see Garrison Headly of BBC Four approaching from the other direction.

Why hadn't she thought to go out the back door?

"Molly Graham!" This came from Jennessee, who was practically out of breath. "What do you have to say about the theft of the harbor funds?" In a heartbeat the microphone was under Molly's chin. "That grant you obtained for the renovation. Have you heard it's been filched?"

"Garrison Headly here in Blackpool reporting on thieves who seem to have absconded with a good deal of money from the coffers of a town whose history is wrapped up in smugglers and piracy. At this moment, I'm with Molly Graham." A second microphone appeared. "Mrs. Graham, we just learned that more than one hundred thousand pounds was pilfered from the harbor restoration project. The stolen money was a big chunk of that green grant you secured for Blackpool from the Sustainable Development Fund."

Molly stared blankly ahead.

"Would you care to comment?" Headly asked.

Again she wished that she'd never filled in that first line on the grant application.

"Mrs. Graham…" Jennessee prompted.

"From what I understand," Molly began, "it was eighty-six thousand pounds, not one hundred."

"We saw the D.C.I. lead two men away," Jennessee said. "Can you tell us who they were?"

Molly saw Edward scribbling rapidly. The local reporter knew exactly who the two men were.

"I'm sorry, Miss Stanwood," Molly said. "You'll have to get that information from the police."

"It were Dennis Carteret and his cohort, Percy Lethbridge. That's who it were." Barnaby Stone had slogged his way up the sidewalk, wearing a Barnaby's Bait T-shirt, orange this time, with a smear of something near the waist. "Jacks nabbed both of them. Saw the Judyscuffer give old Dennis the what-for."

Judyscuffer—lady cop, Molly translated automatically. Sergeant Krebs. Molly's chest felt tight. Where had Barnaby come from? The docks? Were more people on their way over? A heartbeat later that question was answered in the affirmative when she spotted a gaggle of Green Gladiators. Michael tried to part the throng so the two of them could escape.

"Percy—Percy Lethbridge," Barnaby continued. "That's who Paddington stuffed into the back of his car. The Judyscuffer took Dennis. Word is they stole the money. Can't dredge 'cause of the sunken ship. Now they can't build 'cause the dosh's gone from their precious harbor fund. Guess ain't nothing going to happen to the harbor." He smiled widely, genuinely pleased with the turn of events.

Questions swirled, from the reporters mainly, but a few from the growing number of townsfolk. Jennessee's higher-pitched voice was the easiest to make out. But all of it sounded like hornets buzzing in a nest.

"Calm down, all of you," Michael said.

Molly dug her fingernails into her palms and thrust her hands into her pockets.

More questions came at her.

"Enough!" She felt certain she was glaring, so she relaxed her face and exhaled slowly. "I want to know what's going on, too. I have no authority to comment on anything beyond the grant, and—"

"Then can you comment specifically *on* the grant… on the money stolen from the fund?" The question came from Headly.

"It's up to the police to determine if something has been stolen," she answered.

"You mentioned eighty-six thousand," Jennessee said.

"I really can't comment—"

"But eighty-six thousand is a comment," Jennessee insisted. "That means you know something. How much money was stolen. Maybe who stole it. Do you, Molly Graham, know who took the money? Can you confirm the amount that was taken?"

"A victory for the Green!" Weymouth piped up. "A victory for the harbor and the world!"

Instantly the news cameras swung on him, Jennessee and Headly aiming their microphones in his direction.

Barnaby looked perturbed that the focus had shifted, and he turned to the man behind him—Horsey.

"Go green!" a woman next to Weymouth shouted. "Go, go, go green!"

"Doomed from the beginning, this project was," Barnaby called out. "The planning board couldn't be mithered to look at all the angles. And now see what's happened!" He pumped his fist in the air like a winning prize fighter. "The project will stall."

"Go green!"

"A victory for the Green Gladiators!" Weymouth shouted.

"A victory for Blackpool!" Barnaby corrected.

"A victory for the world!" someone yelled.

Headly stepped close to Molly. "Mrs. Graham, do you think the construction will grind to a halt because of the missing money?"

She took a few steps toward the café door. Michael opened it for her. "No, I do not."

Molly glanced over at the crowd. Was that Arliss sidling up to Weymouth?

"Could you elaborate?"

"There's still money in the fund," Molly said. She wished she'd paid more attention to what she was wearing today. She'd pulled on jeans, faded at the thighs and slightly frayed at the bottoms, and a lightweight sweater, one of her favorites but a bit nubby. Not attire for television, certainly. Lord, she hadn't even bothered with makeup today. But, then, she'd come down to see about the sunken ship, not to appear on the nightly news. "There's enough money to continue work that's already started. And I have every confidence that any missing money will be returned or reimbursed."

"Really?" Headly's eyebrows rose. "So you *do* know something about the money? Who took it, Mrs. Graham?"

"That's for the police," she repeated.

"Go green!" It had become a chant now. Barnaby's coarse words were lost in the mix, as was Arliss's deep voice calling for "order." The sound bounced off the brick facade behind her and seemed to travel through the sidewalk and rumble beneath her feet. "Go green! Go green! Go Green Gladiators!"

Finally, blessedly, a familiar whistle sounded, announcing the presence of a Blackpool constable.

Headly turned to look into the crowd and Molly squeezed past him and back into the café. She and Michael threaded their way through the tables, sidestepping a waitress, who gaped openmouthed when people spilled in after them. Molly and Michael made straight for the back door.

Once in the alley, they headed into the heart of the little town.

"Let's focus on something other than the money, hmm? Do you think it's a coincidence that the body was found at the same location as the ransom drop?" Michael asked.

"Maybe Clark Partridge *was* the kidnapper! Or, rather, one of them."

"It does seem improbable that he just stumbled across the kidnapper at the very remote drop point and then was killed because he'd witnessed the money-grab," Michael said.

"I agree. That would be too much of a coincidence. It's more likely that Clark Partridge was one of the kidnappers, and his partner, or partners, killed him so the ransom money wouldn't have to be shared."

"We have to tell the D.C.I. about this."

"Naturally, Michael, but he'll be figuring it out himself soon, anyway. Dennis and Percy will be talking to him about the kidnapping now." She stopped and leaned against the brick, Michael so close to her that she could feel his breath on her face. "And then there's the question of what's happened to poor Rosamund. I know how worried Dennis must be, but he should have gone to the police in the first place. Keeping silent hasn't kept his daughter safe."

"At least the D.C.I. will probably tie Partridge to the kidnapping now," Michael concluded. "From there the police will figure out who Partridge's accomplice was—"

"—or accomplices—"

"—and ferret out where Rosamund is."

Michael kissed her forehead. "I pray she's still alive, though I worry that might not be the case."

"Clark Partridge is dead," Molly said. "If the kidnapper would kill his partner, why not also murder the victim?"

"I suppose we could go back home and let the D.C.I. sort through this."

"I suppose we could," Molly said.

A few minutes later, however, they strolled into Havana Haven.

"I don't suppose you're here to buy anything," Sandra said.

Michael picked out a few magazines and put them on the counter. As she rang them up, he asked, "About Clark Partridge—"

"The Husky wintergreen man…" Molly prompted.

"The guy you think might be dead?"

"Yes, him," Michael said. "When he came in here, did he ever have any friends with him?"

"A girlfriend once or twice. Mostly came in with a guy. Same age. Could pass for brothers, those two. Except Clark's pal didn't favor chewing tobacco." Sandra smiled slyly. "He bought wrapping papers."

"Do you have his phone number?" Michael stuffed the magazines under his arm.

"Better than that," Sandra replied. "Last time he was in, he used a credit card. So if you want, I can give you his address, too."

"Hungry?" Michael asked Molly as they exited the shop. "It's half past five and I'm starving already. The time's flown today."

"And not in a good way," she said. "Dinner? Sure. Why don't we tell Iris that we're going to eat out tonight?"

"But before dinner, let's take a drive by this address." Michael held up the paper Sandra had given him.

CHAPTER FIFTEEN

THERE WERE TWO EMPTY parking spaces in the apartment complex's lot, and though the sign said Tenants Only, Molly and Michael pulled in.

2B, that was what Sandra the tobacconist had written on the paper. 2B, Nick Atkinson.

Michael beat Molly up the steps, his long legs propelling him faster. He waited at the top. "I suppose we should have phoned the D.C.I. first."

"I suppose."

Michael started for the apartment door, and then pulled out his mobile. He made a quick call, leaving a message with whoever was at the police station's front desk.

"Doing your civic duty?" Molly asked.

"Looking to avoid Paddington yelling at us later," he answered.

The doorbell didn't work, so Michael knocked.

And knocked.

They were about to leave when it finally opened. The man blinked as if he'd just woken up. He appeared gaunt, his hair the color of red clay, long and stringy— a tangled mop—and his face had several days' growth of beard. He rubbed at his eyes and swung his bleary gaze from Michael to Molly.

"What do you want?" Even his voice sounded tired. "Who are you?"

"Nick Atkinson?" Molly asked.

"What of it?"

"You're a friend of Clark Partridge?"

Atkinson started to close the door, but Michael leaned against it.

"What'd Party do? Does he owe you some money? I don't cover none of his debts."

"You were flatmates, right?" Molly queried.

"What of it?" Atkinson's expression softened a little. "Sometimes. On and off. Not since he hit me, though. I tossed him out."

"So you haven't seen him lately?" Michael proposed.

"No. And no, I don't know where you can find him." Atkinson pushed the door closed just as a police van pulled into the lot.

"About that dinner?" Michael prompted.

THEY'D SETTLED ON a place on the edge of town. Molly wanted to be far enough from the harbor that she couldn't see the construction or any of the protestors who might still be parading around. She put the top of her car down and the early evening sun warmed her face nicely. Michael was going to meet her at the restaurant.

She took the long route, figuring Michael would get there first and ask for a table. Scattered amid the trees were low, broken walls from houses of centuries past. The area was old, Molly knew, having found references to it in the library dating back to the 1500s and mentioning William the Conqueror, Tancred the Fleming and the Abbot of Whitby.

Molly eased the Mini Cooper over an old railway track. Blackpool used to have a train station, but it had closed some decades past, and the route now served as a bicycle and hiking path. Molly had ridden it with Michael a few times, but didn't find it challenging enough. She preferred their hikes by the cliffs.

She saw Michael's Land Rover in the lot, which was full, so she chose a place a few blocks away.

They sat by a bay window at a table with a pale yellow linen tablecloth accented with a band of satin trim.

"I should be dressed nicer for this restaurant," she said. There was no "fancier" spot in Blackpool, and it was only open on weekends, save during tourist season.

"Nicer? You're beautiful," Michael said. "And you're dressed just fine."

"I look like I'm ready to go out and weed the garden." She stretched her foot out under the table and rubbed his ankle.

Though Molly considered her husband a steak-and-potatoes guy, tonight he ordered the corn-fed free range chicken, coq au vin, and deconstructed *boulangère* potatoes with red wine. She selected the organic salmon with buttered greens, white asparagus and caviar. They agreed to split a caramelized crème brûlée afterward.

Michael reached across the table and took her hand. "I got a call on my mobile on the way here. The archaeologist is coming in tonight by private plane and is diving tomorrow on that ship. I'm invited."

"I hope you said yes."

"Well…" Michael tapped at the edge of the dessert plate. "I thought it would be impolite to turn him down. Maybe you could come, too."

She smiled and shook her head. "I've other plans. So tell me about this archaeologist."

"He'll be here only one or two days from what I understand. He's going to Liverpool after this, but he's coming back later with a team and more equipment. I probably won't be able to join him then—get in the way and all of that, especially if they're trying to recover things. So I'm taking advantage of tomorrow's invite."

"You'll enjoy it."

"You could entertain yourself with some of your mystery books, you know. Leave the murder and kidnapping to the police, though I don't need to tell you that. D.C.I. Paddington is quite experienced."

"Not my nature to let something go," she returned.

"You're like a bulldog that's got hold of an old sock and won't relinquish it."

She gave him a surprised look.

"I didn't mean that you *resemble* a bulldog. You're ravishing."

"It's a puzzle, Michael."

"I know, and once started, you won't rest until all the pieces are in the right places."

The waiter poured them another glass of wine, then Michael told him to take the bottle away, since they both had to drive.

"Normally the death of someone like Clark Partridge wouldn't catch my interest. But I'm convinced it's tied to the grant money somehow, which is tied to me."

They finished the crème brûlée, which Molly pronounced "heavenly."

"So you want to figure out who was working with Partridge, right? Who kidnapped Rosamund."

"I think I'll start with Weymouth," Molly said. "He's so desperate to stop the renovation, so convinced this is bad for the environment, that he might stoop to kidnapping."

"Maybe."

"Or what about Stefan Draghici?"

Michael shook his head. "He's after Romanian gold, not harbor money. A hundred and fifty thousand is a fortune, but not the fortune he's looking for."

"Barnaby Stone, Clement Horsey…neither wants to

spend their own money on the renovation, and both opposed the plan and spoke out against Dennis Carteret. I remember them protesting his selection for the planning board."

Michael leaned back in the chair. He stretched his legs under the table and this time gently rubbed her ankle. "I'd vote they're both involved. Clement's the smarter of the two. Barnaby's all bluster. I wouldn't put a kidnapping scheme past him, but I'm not sure he's a killer."

"I am not convinced about that," she mused. "His eyes are dark and mean."

Michael signaled the waiter for the check. "What about Percy Lethbridge? What if he did this for money? What if he's behind everything and fooled his friend Dennis?"

"I spent hours with him on more than one weekend when I was putting the grant application together. His eyes—"

"Weren't dark and mean."

"No."

Michael pulled a credit card from his wallet and made a notation for a tip on the check, passing both to the waiter.

"You always look for the good in people, dearest. But there are a few things you don't know about Percy Lethbridge."

Molly cocked her head. "Do tell."

"He's a womanizer, for one."

"A rumor—"

"Well, rumor is that he's been blackmailed, held to his own ransom, so to speak, by various women. It's pretty common knowledge that he's had indiscretions on occasion. Supposedly he pays up to keep his marriage intact. I don't know if he loves his wife, but he loves his position in the community. And he's a clever chap…when he's not thinking with his John Thomas."

"Are you saying—"

"I'm saying it is one very distinct possibility he was involved with the ransom demand. And I'll wager that D.C.I. Paddington is looking closely at that angle."

"But Dennis and Percy are friends. I can't see Percy—"

"Desperation will drive people to very bad deeds, love."

"Interesting."

"Now, about those after-dinner plans…"

"I'll follow you home. I'm parked a couple of blocks away."

"See you in a few minutes."

They kissed and he went out the front entrance. She went out the back and walked the few blocks to her car. Leaning on the Mini Cooper was Esma Draghici.

Molly reached for her keys. "What can I do for you, Esma?"

"It is not you I want to talk to. Your husband. Is Michael Graham coming along?"

So Esma had assumed Michael had ridden with her.

"It's just me, Esma."

The woman was regal-looking and proud. A little taller than Molly, her dark hair was swept back in a ponytail that reached to the small of her back. Her fingers were thick with rings, none of which seemed valuable, and large silver hoops hung from her ears. She smelled of spice and tea, and she wore no makeup, though her eyelashes were enviably long and curling.

"Then you give your husband Michael a message from me."

"Of course."

"You tell your husband to stop looking for the gold. It belongs to Stefan and me, to our family. There were coins found in Blackpool not too long ago. It was in the news, and that is why we are here."

"Michael isn't—"

"He looks for our gold, Mrs. Graham. Everyone knows he looks. This town, it is small, and there are no secrets. You tell him to stop."

"Because you're afraid he might find it." Molly wished she could have swallowed those words. She hadn't intended to voice the sentiment.

"You get him to back off. And you urge him to admit that the gold should belong to Stefan and me and our family. You make him tell the paper."

Was Michael on to something? Had he discovered an important clue about the gold's whereabouts?

"What is it you think Michael has found?"

"Nothing yet," Esma spat. "But I want to make sure it stays nothing. That gold, it is ours. You understand?"

"I'll give Michael your message."

The Gypsy woman pushed off from the car and watched Molly get in and drive away.

She thought Esma's eyes had seemed dark and mean.

CHAPTER SIXTEEN

JENNESSEE, HEADLY from BBC Four and a few other reporters were at the harbor to record the arrival of the archaeologist, Professor Algernon Hume-Thorson, who'd taken a private plane to get here.

Michael met him on the dock. Hume-Thorson wasn't what he'd expected. The title *professor* had always conjured up an image of an older, scholarly man with salt-and-pepper hair and well-trimmed beard. But Hume-Thorson was in his mid-thirties, trim and rather muscular. His face was all angles and planes, and his wide-set eyes were a bright blue that matched the sport shirt he was wearing.

It was a small world; the professor had turned out to be a computer-game aficionado and a fan of Michael's work. That was the reason Michael had been invited for the dive on the shipwreck. Michael was glad for the distraction. He could feel that the models held a clue to the gold, but he couldn't figure it out. And Molly's relayed message from the Draghicis had unsettled him, though it wouldn't put him off for long.

He'd brought his own gear for the dive; it was already loaded on the boat that would take them to the dredging platform. They were going to dive from there, since it was close to the ship and afforded a little more privacy than the dock.

Sergeant Krebs maintained order at the docks this morning, though the crowd that gathered was more curious than rowdy, and there was no sign of Barnaby, Horsey or a single Green Gladiator.

Construction continued on a few of the businesses. The sounds of sanders, hammers and planks of wood dropping competed with the buzz of conversations and the cries of the seabirds circling overhead.

"Very pleased to meet you, Michael," Hume-Thorson said.

"Likewise, Professor."

"Call me Algernon, please." His voice was crisp and had a "Brummie" flavor in the way he pronounced vowels, indicating he was from Birmingham or around there.

"All right, Algernon," Michael said. The professor's handshake was firm, his fingers callused.

"I told your Mrs. Hogan I would say something to the planning board and the press here. So give me a moment."

He turned and addressed the assemblage. "I am what you call an underwater archaeologist or maritime archaeologist because I concentrate on salt water," he began. "I specialize in studying people and their cultures by analyzing physical remains found in the sea. My science traces its roots to salvagers who explored shipwrecks and downed aircraft. In this instance, it appears we're going to study an old schooner."

Jennessee and Headly started their barrage of questions, but the professor waved them away.

"Maritime archaeology can tell us a lot about Blackpool. Sunken ships are a time capsule, if you will, a cache of artifacts humans valued at a particular moment in time. Many ships are important discoveries not because of how they were wrecked but because of their function in their own days. Was the ship the first of its design? Was it a marvel of naval warfare? The United States's *Hunley* submarine was both historic and unique. The *Holland Five* was marked significant because of the British navy's foray into submarine warfare. And it is not just about the ships, it's about the sea itself. When we study a wreck, we learn about changes in the ocean due to climate or earthquakes or the human toll."

"What do you hope to find here?" This came from Arliss, her white-gloved hands fluttering like birds.

"I always hope to find something amazing," he answered. "And I am rarely disappointed. It will, however, depend on how much sediment is over the ship, and the temperatures of the water. The colder and darker, the more will be preserved, such as leathers, fabrics and the wood of the ship itself. Every site is different, and more hazardous than working on dry land, of course. Fortunately, this is a relatively shallow dive. There's a strong tide here, so that's against us. But the weather looks promising, which will help. I usually have a lot more equipment with me, but we're under time constraints and so we're, as they say, 'making do.' I understand that visibility here could be poor because of the disturbed silt. That will make everything a little more difficult. The wreck is also subject to the currents, which can break it up and scatter artifacts…if it hasn't been looted by earlier divers. The piddocks might get to it, if they haven't already."

"Piddocks?" Arliss asked.

"Piddocks—angelwings," he replied. "They look like clams. A piddock's shell has ridges, or teeth, that are used to grind away substances such as water-soddened hulls, so the creature can make burrows. They burrow their entire lives."

"Back to the shipwreck," Jennessee urged. "What if there's treasure? Will you bring it up?"

He chuckled. "I don't anticipate bringing anything up today, no. The artifacts, if any exist, will be recovered in time. Everything will be removed in stages and carefully preserved."

He tugged a folder out of his satchel. "Let me share some photographs with you. The dredging team took these and sent them to my computer yesterday. They're what got me to drop everything and come out here. This outline could be a bell. That will help us identify the ship, I should think. But here's the interesting part. Look here and here."

Jennessee pushed in close, wedging herself between

Michael and the professor. She thrust her microphone under the archaeologist's chin and motioned for her cameraman to get a shot. "What, exactly, are we looking at?"

"This gaping hole. My initial assessment is that this ship was deliberately sunk. See the damage done to the hull? The dredging equipment didn't do that."

Michael instantly thought of Blackpool's Maritime Museum and some of the shipwrecks and artifacts displayed there. He was familiar with the stories of brigands who set traps for ships to run aground on the shoals, where they were easy prey for looting.

"So someone sent this ship to the bottom of your harbor on purpose," Hume-Thorson said. "Who and why? That's a puzzle I hope to solve, but I don't have much time to do it in. Now, if you'll excuse us. Perhaps we can all chat over a pint or two once we call quits, eh?"

He caught Michael's attention and gestured to the ladder leading to the boat. "I've only got until tomorrow morning here because of a lecture series I've committed to in Liverpool."

Michael spotted Rohan on the fringes. His friend was supposed to be working, but Rohan seemed distracted, alternately looking at the dredging platform, the row of sailboats in the harbor and Hume-Thorson. He noticed Michael and flashed a toothy grin, mouthing "all fruit's ripe." Michael returned the smile before climbing down the ladder and into the boat.

It didn't take them long to reach the dredging platform and don their scuba gear.

"If I decide a crew should come in, Michael, they'll clear the site properly. I only work with the best. And I'm likely to recommend that all dredging stop—for months, if need be. Once the site is cleared enough for further exploration, they'll put out a reference grid. I'll try to come back at that point—rearrange my schedule if I must."

"A grid? What's that for?" In the back of his mind Michael saw the makings of another computer game, one where the players combed the sea floor for wrecks and were tasked with bringing up the most artifacts.

"The grid will be used to reference different areas of the site."

Michael nodded, getting a good mental picture. "But we can dive today without any of that?"

"Of course. We're dressed for it, aren't we? I want to take a look and see how much trouble we should go to over this. We need to take plenty of pictures." He displayed a state-of-the-art digital camera.

"And then…" Michael made a mental note to ask him later where to get one of those cameras.

"Well, if the wreck hasn't been looted already, we'll…loot it." He chuckled. "Actually, we'll catalog everything and determine what should be brought up. And then when we're finished, Blackpool can dredge its harbor."

"And the longer it takes to assess the wreck, the happier the Green Gladiators will be."

The professor tipped his head in question.

"I'll tell you all about it over a pint or two."

"Or three," Algernon chuckled.

Minutes later, they were in another world, several meters deep and angling toward the site of the wreck.

Michael loved diving and wished Molly was more interested in it. She'd come on a few dives with him, and seemed to enjoy it. But she didn't share his passion nor was she interested in staying down as long. She did, however, mention giving it another try in a more tropical location—like the Bahamas. He hoped she was making progress on the murder of Clark Partridge and the kidnapping. He was torn; he wanted to be sharing the mystery with her. But he also wanted to be here.

The water was murky, and Michael realized the silt had been stirred up by the dredgers.

Algernon and Michael closed in on the wreck, another diver joining them. The man had come on the plane with Hume-Thorson, and Michael had been introduced to him, but he couldn't remember his name: Drew or Doug? He'd apologize and ask later. The man had a camera similar to Algernon's.

Michael's eyes grew wide when he saw the wreck. It was a huge ship.

The professor pointed to what looked like an

enormous gun mounted to some sort of a swivel on the port side, a broad circle of iron that was rusted and encrusted with barnacles. The water and the silt distorted the size of the gun, making it appear larger. Still, it was similar in size to what a pirate would have had in decades past, a necessary weapon for a ship carrying ill-gotten gains.

The foremast was thick but it had been snapped like a telephone pole in a typhoon. Perhaps a great storm had taken the ship under rather than the brigands notorious for luring vessels onto the shoals. But the professor had mentioned evidence that the ship had been sunk on purpose.

The ship, which had been schooner rigged, was relatively intact. The prow was notably damaged where the dredging equipment had struck it. The soddened wood had broken easily, but put up just enough resistance that the dredging crew had noticed something was amiss. The three men swam through the hole now and increased the brightness of their lights. The interior of the hull possessed an otherworldly beauty, yet at the same time was grotesque and haunting. The sea had claimed it, coating objects with an algae-slime that sucked in the light, muting everything. Small fish darted above and below them, silvery flashes like miniature shooting stars.

Michael recalled several lines from Ariel's Song in Shakespeare's *The Tempest:*

Full fathom five thy father lies;
Of his bones are coral made;
Those are pearls that were his eyes;
Nothing of him that doth fade,
But doth suffer a sea-change;
Into something rich and strange.

Michael realized this dive was a good distraction
for him, since he'd been thinking of nothing but the
treasure, the murder and kidnapping up to this point.
Not to mention Molly's troubles. All that was in the
back of his mind now, and he had to push it away and
focus on the ship. Maybe time away from the mysteries would help him take a fresh approach later with
Molly.

They caught sight of large kettles that must have
been used for cooking—they had stumbled upon the
galley. Even from the inside Michael could tell it was
a particularly broad-decked ship. There were three
main interior decks, and they explored each briefly,
pointing out features with rudimentary hand signals.

Michael stared at the grated hatchways between
decks. The spaces were so small, no more than a foot
or two wide. A variety of rusted leg irons and fetters
were everywhere. And there were lots of bones, too.
Many people had died when the ship went down.

Algernon held a hand up, fingers spread, signaling
five, then followed that gesture by rounding his fingers
to form zeros.

Five hundred…or more, the professor indicated by spreading his arms apart.

Five hundred or more.

That's how many slaves the ship had held. The professor believed the ship had been a slaver.

The archaeologists took pictures of everything.

The slaves must have been kept close together like livestock. They could hardly have sat up or changed position once they were put in here. How could it have been possible for so many people to exist, packed in here like sardines, wedged together in spaces with three-foot-high ceilings? The heat and the stench must have been incredible. Michael fought to keep from gagging just thinking about it. No light would have reached down here, and the air would have been fetid.

He prayed that many of the slaves had been off-loaded before the ship sunk, or that they had somehow survived and swam to safety. There didn't look to be enough bones to equal hundreds of slaves…dozens certainly.

Nothing of him that doth fade, But doth suffer a sea-change; Into something rich and strange.

Algernon flashed his light, getting Michael's attention. He aimed the beam at a rack on the wall where several implements had miraculously remained attached.

My God, Michael thought.

There were branding irons and a scourge from

which twisted, rotted leather thongs dangled, ending in now-rusted bits of metal.

He recalled reading an account of a slave ship in the papers at the Maritime Museum. There'd been hundreds of people on it, all ages, all nude, packed like sheep, occasionally allowed the luxury of clean air on deck, indifferent to life or death or pain, some not able to stand. Hell could not be much different, and certainly not any worse, one of the mates had written.

Hell had been uncovered here at the bottom of Blackpool's quiet, silt-filled harbor, Michael thought. Suddenly, his treasure hunt and his undead space game seemed inconsequential.

Algernon tapped him on the shoulder, rousing Michael from his dark mood. The archaeologist indicated his watch and pointed up.

Michael understood; their tanks were running low on oxygen. They'd been down here a long time, though it had seemed like only minutes. They had to surface.

Michael didn't need Algernon's assessment to know that the dredging would be shut down for quite a while.

CHAPTER SEVENTEEN

MOLLY HAD BARELY SLEPT last night, images of Clark Partridge's corpse filling her mind. She thought about his last minutes, and who could have killed him. Atkinson? He looked like a bum, but even in the scant few minutes she'd seen him, he'd come across to her as an honest one.

She'd heard from Iris that he'd been taken in for questioning last night and arrested on some drug charge. Maybe Molly could get in to see him today… as well as Dennis and Percy.

She couldn't let the mystery sit unsolved. Besides, she wanted to talk to D.C.I. Paddington, anyway, and ask if he had any news on the kidnapping.

Coffee did little to shake off her sluggishness, so she took care in applying makeup to hide the dark circles. After appearing on camera yesterday in her frayed clothes, she was going to make a point to dress well…just in case she ran in to one of the reporters.

One stop, she decided, on the way to the jail.

Molly parked in front of Dennis Carteret's house, a sprawling stone-fronted two-level manse. She decided to leave the driveway open in case…in case of what?

The owner of the house was in jail, so he wouldn't be coming home.

There was a bright yellow Twingo in the drive, under a carport.

Whose car was it? Certainly not Dennis's. The man was too tall for something as tiny as the Renault. She couldn't picture him squeezing into it.

Maybe a housekeeper's, she thought. Or some relative taking care of the place and watering the plants.

She went up the front steps, deciding she'd tell whoever was inside that she was going to the jail and wondered if she could take anything for Dennis. What she really wanted to do was take a look around.

Molly had almost given up ringing the bell at the front door when a young woman answered—she was in her early twenties and pretty.

"Rosamund?" Molly fairly shouted the word.

The woman nodded. "Do I know you?"

"The kidnapper let you go!" Molly wanted to reach out and squeeze her, but the woman's hard, dark eyes stopped her.

"I wasn't kidnapped."

"But your father—"

"Do I know you?" Rosamund repeated, irritation thick in her voice.

"I'm Molly Graham. I helped your father and the planning board with—"

"Oh. I've heard of you. What are you doing here?" Rosamund's tone was flat, bordering on rude. It took Molly aback, and for a few moments she said nothing.

"Does your father—"

"Know that I'm safe? Yeah. I saw him at the jail late last night when I got in."

"How? What—"

"I spoke with the constables, too."

Molly felt her mouth drop open.

"So…why did you come to the house?" Rosamund leaned out the door and gave Molly a once-over.

Molly struggled to regain her composure. "I'd like to help your father."

"He could use help." Still her voice was flat.

"Can I come in? Can we talk?"

Rosamund shrugged. Her youthful face was free of makeup, her startling gray eyes unblinking, and her short chestnut colored hair tousled.

"I don't want to talk to you, Mrs. Graham. I don't want to talk to anyone."

"I don't blame you. In fact, I—"

The phone rang shrilly and Rosamund closed her eyes. "It's been doing that all morning. And all last night, ever since I got home."

"Reporters."

Rosamund nodded.

"Mine rings all the time, too." Molly paused. "I haven't been answering it, either."

That seemed to strike a chord. Rosamund stepped back and gestured Molly inside.

"Tea?"

"That would be lovely," Molly said.

"I only have one kind."

"Whatever you have will be fine."

Molly had seen Rosamund around town before and heard that she was headstrong, proud, self-involved… and prone to dating young men her father did not approve of. But Molly didn't see anyone else in the house. She did see an emotionless girl who'd thrown a sweatshirt over the top of her pajamas.

They sat in high-backed upholstered chairs on either side of a low, black walnut table in the living room. The tea was a Darjeeling with a light and pungent flavor and served in stoneware mugs that felt somehow comforting in Molly's hands.

"So…you want to help my dad, right?"

"Yes."

"I'm going down to see him later this morning. They let him call out a little while ago."

"How is he faring?"

Rosamund shrugged, the neck of the baggy sweater slipping down over one shoulder. "All right, I suppose," she said after a moment. "How's he supposed to fare? He's in jail." A touch of defiance surfaced in her eyes. "A baboon he was, thinking I was kidnapped."

Molly inhaled the tea before taking a sip. She'd remember to ask Iris to add Darjeeling tea to her shopping list. "He couldn't reach you. He thought you had been kidnapped. We all thought you had been kidnapped."

"Nobody kidnapped me. That was pretty ridiculous. I just didn't want to be found, you know, not for a few days."

"Where were you?"

"Like I told the D.C.I. last night, I was with some friends. All right—*a* friend, my boyfriend, and we just wanted a little time alone. How was I supposed to know someone would pretend to kidnap me?" She stuck her finger in the tea to test its temperature and then took a swallow. "I said all this to the constables last night. Why am I banging on about it to you now? You're not with the police."

"No, but I am trying to find out what happened. I really do want to help your father."

"Why? Because your neck's on the line?" Rosamund stared at her, unblinking. "Because you're the one who got the money from the government for Blackpool's harbor? The constables told me that's how my dad paid this supposed-kidnapper—with harbor money. Looks bad on you that some of it's gone now. But you're not the one in jail. Dad is."

Molly didn't say anything. She looked around the small room, at the Oriental rug on the floor and the framed pictures on the wall. There was a photograph of Rosamund as a tot, sitting on her mother's knee, a puppy on her lap—a poodle mix. Molly recalled Dennis saying his wife had died when Rosamund was a child, and he'd never remarried. Word was that Dennis doted on her, sending her to a school in Manchester, some sort of academy that cost more than a pretty penny.

"The dog's name was Fluffy. Silly name for a dog, don't you think? I didn't get to keep her long. Dad snapped that picture. He took most of the pictures hanging around here. What a fool, believing I'd been kidnapped."

"Don't be angry at your father," Molly said. "He loves you."

"I'm not angry at him." Rosamund drained the rest of her tea. "He probably thinks I am, though. We don't always get along. I'm just…I guess I'm just angry at the situation. Why'd he have to steal? If he was going to pay a fake kidnapper, couldn't he have come up with enough money of his own? He's not poor, you know." She thumped the empty mug down on the table and hunched forward, resting her elbows on her knees.

"I'm sure he's not poor, but the kidnapper wanted the money right away." Molly regarded the girl, trying to decipher the emotions rolling across her face. "The kidnapper had to know you were out of town, and wouldn't be coming back for a while."

"So I went off on a jolly to London. So what? I'm old enough, and more than a few folks knew I was gone. So I didn't tell Dad where I was the whole time. I'm old enough for that, too. I don't have to account for where I am at every moment of the day. Hell, I used to be away for months at a time—"

"At the academy."

"Yes. Months at a time, and no one thought I was kidnapped then."

"This was different, Rosa—"

"I'm twenty-two, not two."

Molly let an odd silence settle between them. She heard a car go by outside. The phone rang again then stopped. From an upstairs room came the faint sounds of radio.

"It's not all reporters calling," Rosamund said. "Some folks in town are upset, calling Dad a thief, not having the courtesy to say it to his face but telling me, instead. One had the nerve to blame it on me 'cause I'd gone on a holiday." She picked up the mug again, and Molly expected her to go into the kitchen for more hot water. But she sat there, running her thumbs along the rim. "But you're not accusing him."

"No," Molly said. *I don't have to. He confessed to me that he stole the money.*

"You're a good sort, even for an American. And I'm glad I let you in. Nice to have a sympathetic ear to bend, you know?" She shrugged again—a habit, Molly guessed. "I can't say as I blame them, really— being upset about the money, I mean. Arliss Hogan is flipping her wig, Dad said. But they should be angry at whoever really stole it."

"You mean whoever claimed you had been kidnapped?"

"Yeah, I've been thinking about that a lot. Trying to guess what barmpot might have done such a thing."

"Any ideas?"

"I don't have a clue. Wish I did. D.C.I. Paddington hoped I could point him in the right direction. But if wishes were fishes, like I told the D.C.I., I'd have several aquariums full." She smiled, but only briefly. "Do you?"

Molly cocked her head.

"Do you have any ideas? Heard you're something of an amateur sleuth, or so Dad says."

"I'm a grant writer, actually. But I have an uncle who is a detective, and when I was younger he'd spin stories laced with international intrigue. They always excited me. My husband jokes that if I hadn't taken to grant writing I would have been a detective."

"But not in Blackpool," Rosamund said flatly. "Not much intriguing happens here, except for Dad stealing the harbor dosh." She tipped her head back. "I don't always get along with him. Hell, he doesn't always get along with me. But it's not right they should toss him in jail when he was only trying to help me."

"He broke the law, taking the money." Molly wished she could have swallowed those words. She hadn't meant to say them aloud.

"He's got a good barrister, and Dad's promised to pay the money back. He's going to sell his business down at the harbor. That'll more than make up for what he stole…what him and Percy stole. The barrister thinks he might get Dad off without any jail time, just probation. Depends on the court, though. Maybe he'll do a year or two. Percy will probably get less." She frowned. "I suppose maybe I should've let Dad know where I was in London. None of this would have happened. My friends there could've told him where I was. He just didn't call the right ones, I guess."

The phone rang again and Rosamund waited until voice mail picked it up.

Molly finished her tea and set the mug on the table. "Did you know someone named Clark Partridge?"

Rosamund blinked in surprise. "The D.C.I. asked me that same thing last night. Said he was dead, right where Dad and Percy dropped the ransom money." She paused when the phone rang again. "I should just pull the plug on the damn thing. Yeah, I knew who Party Partridge was. Not quite in my social circle, if you catch my drift. Face like a welder's bench, always low on quid."

"And he knew you?"

"Sure. Blackpool's a small place, all things considered. Hard not to know anyone who's lived here a few years."

"Could he have set this up?"

"Stage a fake kidnapping? That's the D.C.I.'s theory, I suppose. But I don't see how he could have known I was on holiday." She tugged on her lip. "Unless a mutual friend told him. But I'd never have guessed we had any mutual friends."

"About those friends…friend…you stayed with in London—"

"I gave the list to the D.C.I."

Molly wanted the list, too, but decided not to press Rosamund. She could try to get it from Paddington, or she might use it as an excuse to come back and see the Carteret girl later.

"I should be going." She looked at her watch.

The phone rang again.

"Damn. I am going to unplug it."

It stopped then started up once more.

"God, I've come to hate that sound—damnable phone."

"It might be your father calling." Molly followed Rosamund to the front door.

"I'm going down to see him in a little while. After I clean up. Take him some roast lamb and Yorkshire pudding. I figure even my cooking has to be better than what they're serving in jail."

"Tell him to keep his spirits up."

"You should do that yourself," Rosamund said. "It'd be nice if he had some visitors who weren't fixing to lynch him."

CHAPTER EIGHTEEN

"I WANT YOU TO KNOW, Algernon, that I appreciate being allowed along on this second dive." Michael donned his wet suit on the dredging platform. He'd had nearly two hours to dry out after this morning's foray.

None of the dredgers were present this afternoon, and most of them had already gone home. Arrangements were being made to move the platform and other equipment to another job site up the coast. Though some parts of Blackpool Harbor could be dredged without endangering the shipwreck, a decision had been made to postpone the project until any relics had been brought up and it was determined whether the ship—or pieces of it—could be preserved.

Alfie was on the platform with Michael and Algernon, along with Edward, the local newsman, who'd managed to finagle an interview out of the professor. Sergeant Krebs was there as well, keeping watch to make sure none of the locals were diving. She walked stiffly back and forth across the platform, once tripping on a cable and tangling her feet so that Michael had to help her up. She was not pleased she'd embarrassed herself, and her eyes were like daggers.

"I will admit, Michael, that in the many years I've been doing this, you're the first person I've invited down who has not been a part of the team," the professor said. "Even on land digs archaeologists are squeamish about letting a nonprofessional have a go at a site. Oh, students are allowed…though mainly because we have no choice in the matter."

"I'm honored then."

The professor gave him a lopsided grin. "Just be mindful, like before, not to disturb anything. Can't have the site compromised. And from our initial look this morning, I'd say it's a relatively untouched wreck—untouched by human hands, in any event. The fish and piddocks having a nibble is to be expected."

"Piddocks." Michael liked the sound of the word; he'd have to use it in a game.

"Discovering a slaver as intact as this is, well, that's quite the find. Let's hope we can reveal who she is… was."

"The bell?"

"Sent the pictures off an hour ago. Hopefully the partial number and the configuration of the schooner should help. I thought I might have heard back by now, but I've learned in this business that everything takes longer than you want it to." He zipped up his wet suit and adjusted his tank. "I see us doing just two more dives today—not bringing anything up, though. Just recording. I wish I didn't have this Liverpool commitment. But I'll be back when I'm finished there. Maybe you can dive down again with me then."

The other man with them—Drew, he'd confirmed—had a writing tablet and pen designed for use underwater. Michael wanted to buy himself one of those, too, along with a camera like the professor's. He'd already written down the make and model.

"Shall we?" Algernon nodded to his assistant, who went over the side. "Mind the store for us, please," he said to Krebs. Then he went over, too.

Michael followed a few moments later.

Again he found himself wishing Molly could be a part of this, but he doubted very much that the professor would have agreed to let a second novice come along, one with even fewer hours in scuba gear than Michael. He wondered how she was making out with her sleuthing.

The silt had settled some and the sea was calmer, so it was a little easier to make out details. The ship looked even larger, and he guessed it was at least two hundred and fifty feet long and more than forty feet across. Its depth? Michael couldn't hazard a guess because so much of it was under silt. They swam around the boat, slowly, Michael keeping a respectful distance back from the two marine archaeologists. At the same time, he didn't want to miss anything.

There was definitely a computer game here, one that would have the players competing to find the most wrecks, ferret out the ships' and captains' identities and try to recover artifacts…. His mind churned with all the possibilities. Submerged! Perfect name to call it.

On the earlier dive he thought the ship was a three-masted schooner, but swimming above it now, with the water so much clearer, he could tell she actually had boasted five. He saw no name embellished anywhere, the sea having eaten away the paint and some of the finest details.

She must have been beautiful in her day, he realized, and the captain must've been proud to have command of her. Then his thoughts turned dark when he recalled the ship's purpose—bringing slaves from Africa to labor in Europe and America.

The two marine archaeologists seemed to be concentrating on the top deck. Michael hovered above them.

He saw the professor take more pictures of the bell and of the configuration where the wheel had been. It had clearly broken loose.

Amidships, the damage was slight, but when they reached the bilge, it looked as though a cannonball had penetrated. The ship's starboard was covered with rubble from what Michael surmised to be a natural breakwater that had collapsed.

The stern was detached from the hull in one spot and half-buried in the silt, but they could see rust-encrusted iron bands on the forward face. Algernon had explained between dives that the ship had a saddle mast step running across the breadth of its bow, and he had shown Michael a drawing Drew had made that revealed a hole where the base of a mast had been.

The two specialists found the stump of the mast at the bottom of the hull, its position confirming that the wreck was a schooner. Michael could tell even from his vantage point that the frames were moulded and sided, the turn of the bilge rounded and the planking in relatively good condition, especially at the bow. A lot of the rigging remained, as well.

After a couple of hours they took a break and relaxed on the dredging platform. Beggar gulls circled, hoping for a bite of sandwich. Krebs munched on potato chips and occasionally held one out for the gulls to swoop down and snatch from her fingers.

Was she smiling? Enjoying herself? Michael thought a pleasant expression had cracked the sergeant's otherwise stoic face.

"Quite the find. Quite the find." Algernon looked as giddy as a school kid who'd just received straight As on his report. "Did you notice the timbers, Michael? Two of them scarfed together? Well made indeed. We couldn't get under anything, actually—the ship's so stuck in the silt. But all indications are that it has a false keel in the bow."

"Could that be a secret compartment?" Michael asked. "Like a false bottom in a chest?"

Algernon scratched at his chin. "Well, I suppose

you could use it for such a purpose. If you wanted to hide something." He pursed his lips in thought. "I suppose you could at that. Now I'll have to check, see if historically it was done." His expression grew wistful. "She would have been quite the beauty in her day, no expense spared. The planks are thick. They would have been solid, and fastened with iron spikes and bolts."

The professor used terms Michael had no clue about—pintle, cathead, camber, cofferdam, fiddley, jack crosstree, timenoguy—but not wanting to seem too much of a landlubber, Michael didn't ask the meanings. He decided a trip to the bookstore or an online shopping spree was in order to add to his collection of reference books.

On the third and final dive of the day, when it was late afternoon, they swam into what appeared to be the captain's quarters, the largest living space they'd ventured into, and with traces of opulence.

The room was so eerie, Michael thought, as if the old timbers were drinking in the light from the special lanterns the divers held and letting the shadows reign. Ghosts seemed to be dancing around them as pieces of tapestries that had hung on the walls undulated in the water, ephemeral and haunting.

Then their beams of light illuminated the skeleton behind the desk. Pieces of cloth clung to the bones, and a thick gold chain hung about its neck.

The heavy desk had been bolted to the floor, the

chair rotting around the bones. The archaeologists took more pictures while Michael stared at the skeleton.

Were these the remains of the captain? That was Michael's first guess since this must have been the captain's cabin. The skull looked like that of a full-grown man, and the gold chain indicated someone of importance. It could also have been the first mate or boatswain's mate. No dental records back then, so he doubted Algernon would be able to positively identify the bones.

They surfaced and returned to the dredging platform. Sergeant Krebs was gone, replaced by a younger constable who was seated on a folding chair, working on a crossword puzzle.

"Do you know much about the slave trade around here?" Algernon asked Michael. "Around Blackpool specifically?"

"No, unfortunately," Michael answered. He started pulling off the scuba gear.

"I'm passing familiar with the history of it in general," Algernon said. "So-called legitimate business-men who dealt in sugar and rum developed ties with slavers in West Africa. These slavers captured men, women, even children, and shipped them to the Caribbean and America. In the Caribbean they'd trade the slaves for rum sometimes, but often just money. But how that ties in to Blackpool and this area, I have no idea."

Michael shrugged into a long-sleeve T-shirt and

ran his fingers through his hair. He noticed the young constable had put his puzzle book away and was listening.

"From what I've read, and what Alfie from the Maritime Museum has told me," Michael said, "British companies and ships were involved. But in…oh, I think it was in 1807, the Slave Trade Act was enacted, making any participation illegal. Trading in slaves, even simply transporting them for an American company, was criminal. British captains who continued the practice were dubbed pirates. A year later, supposedly, America outlawed the slave trade."

"But it didn't outlaw slavery."

"No, it didn't abolish slavery, and the market thrived secretly."

Algernon slipped into a polo shirt and put a linen jacket over it. "I'd like to think that this ship we've found sailed before 1807."

"But you don't believe that?"

"My gut says no."

Michael put on his socks, grimacing when he saw one was dark blue and the other gray. He'd been in such a hurry this morning that he hadn't turned on the lights in the bedroom when he'd dressed. He quickly slipped on his canvas loafers.

"But you won't know for sure until the ship is identified."

"Right." The professor worked a kink out of his

neck and fixed his gaze on the shore. "But my gut is usually right about ships."

"So maybe she was sunk running from the law."

Algernon didn't say anything for a moment, his attention now drawn to a pair of seagulls squabbling over a scrap of food. Then he said, "Ale? Want to join me for a pint?"

"There's a pub in the marina I like."

"First round is on you."

CHAPTER NINETEEN

ALGERNON TOOK A PULL from his mug. "I favor Boddingtons Pub Ale back home, usually buy it by the case and allow myself one can a day. Or two." He took another drink. "But I think I fancy this better."

Michael took a sip of his. "You won't find this in a can. Draft only, and they make it here."

"Quite nice. Another reason for me to come back. It's a brown ale, right?"

Michael nodded. "They call it English-style brown ale."

"Good thing I'm not flying to Liverpool until early tomorrow morning." He finished the mug and tapped it, signaling for another.

Michael gestured for the barkeep to refill his, too. He'd have to call Molly for a ride home.

"That gold chain around the man's neck." Algernon took another deep gulp. "That will help us identify the captain. And I'm sure that was the captain."

Michael noticed he used the term *man,* rather than *skeleton.* A sign of respect? "Oh?"

"Got a close-up of the fob on it, and the maker's mark."

Michael stared at the red-brown surface of his ale. It smelled good and strong and swirled with all the other aromas in his favorite pub. There was the suggestion of pipe smoke clinging to a few patrons' shirts, along with fresh popcorn—which was always being refilled in baskets on tables and the bar—warring aftershaves and always a touch of the sea air.

"I want you to know I really appreciate you allowing me to dive with you today." Michael was sincere; he'd considered it one of his best experiences since settling in Blackpool. "Everything was amazing, and at the same time horrible. The thought of going down either in a storm or to cannon fire. And worse, the idea of slaving. It's bittersweet—the romance of the sea and the hellishness of mistreating people—"

"Could be more than the five hundred slaves I first estimated."

"And transported as if they were no better than common livestock."

"Thank God some things have changed for the better in this world." Algernon reached for a handful of popcorn and then proceeded to put one piece at a time in his mouth.

Their mood sobered, Michael and the professor listened to the slurred conversation of a pair of fishermen at a nearby table, then straightened when Drew, the other archaeologist, rushed in, searching through the shadowy interior and finally seeing them.

"Professor Algernon!" He twisted his way through

the tight weave of tables, only half of which were occupied this late in the afternoon. He pulled out a chair and sat.

"Ale?" Algernon asked.

"No, but thank you."

"It's very good," the professor went on. "They call it—"

"English-style brown ale," Michael explained.

"All right, I'll have a go."

The professor signaled for the barkeep to bring three more mugs. "Now, what brings you in here all business and bustle? And wearing a cardie—it's too warm for a cardie."

Drew pulled a folded piece of paper out of his front pocket. "The researchers sent us something on the bell."

The professor took the paper and spread it out, then squinted. The small type of the e-mail, coupled by the poor lighting, made it difficult to read.

"May I?" Michael asked. Without taking the paper, he leaned over to get a good look. "It says the registry number verifies a British origin to the schooner, likely named the *Seaclipse,* and owned by one Arnulph de Mounteney."

Algernon drummed his fingers on the table and pushed the paper closer to Michael. "Go on. Go on. Read the rest of it. I didn't bring my glasses."

Michael took a drink of ale to clear his throat. "Mounteney was a young sailor who climbed the ranks quickly and distinguished himself in the Napoleonic Wars, gaining a commission. He was injured in a fight with two crewmen and was booted from the service. He found work on various ships during this time, though records are apparently spotty. He purchased the *Seaclipse,* a known slaver, with money he inherited from an uncle. He crewed it with men who'd spent time in prisons for various offenses and with others who'd served with him in the war. It describes him as dark-eyed, with brown hair, a thin face and athletic build."

"Is there more? Is that it?"

"One more line. It says Mountenay and his entire crew were presumed lost at sea during a storm."

The professor tapped his fingers faster. "Lost at sea, yes, right outside Blackpool here."

"The good news is that the ship at the bottom of our harbor is in relatively good shape," his assistant said, "all things considered."

Michael leaned back in the chair and let out a low whistle. "Alfie will be beside himself with all of this news." He paused a moment. "I'm beside myself."

"Very historical, this find," Algernon said. "Good thing your wife got Blackpool that grant to put the dredging in motion. Otherwise that ship might have rested undiscovered forever." He raised his mug in a toast. "To Molly Graham."

"To Molly Graham," the other two echoed.

"To Molly Graham!" one of the fishermen at a

nearby table joined in. There were a few grumbles from a few patrons opposed to the harbor project, but mostly raised glasses.

"And to the *Seaclipse*," Algernon added.

"To the *Seaclipse*," Michael agreed.

Michael was going to have to call Molly for that ride. He wished she'd been here to learn firsthand about Captain Arnulph de Mounteney. Molly loved puzzles.

The professor had nearly drained his third mug, his eyes red-rimmed, when he announced that he would do his best to cut his Liverpool engagement short. "I'll work out some sort of arrangement with the university. Put in a few days there at least, make some sort of concession, find someone else to fill in the rest of the schedule. I'll be back as soon as possible."

Though not slurred, his words were thick, and Michael knew the ale was affecting him. He wondered if the professor had a drinking problem. It wasn't his business, he decided, at least not unless he became better friends with the man. Besides, he had been wholly sober during the dives, and that was what mattered most.

"The newspapers and TV stations will want to know about this," Michael said. "You met one of our local newsmen, Edward. He covers anything to do with the marina and the harbor. I like him quite a lot."

"By all means let the press in on everything. Might

bring in some more tourists for your lovely little spot on the map. Best alert your head constable, though."

"D.C.I. Maurice Paddington."

"Yes, that's the chap."

Algernon pushed himself away from the table. "Now, if you'll excuse me, I've reached my limit. Passed it, most likely, but I couldn't help myself. Lovely, lovely, this English-style brown ale."

Drew stood. "The hotel has a wireless connection."

"So we'll get back to our researchers, have a snooze and be off in the morning. Oh, and dinner somewhere in there. Do you recommend the Blackpool Café?"

"It's definitely passable," Michael answered.

"Then that's what we'll try."

Michael thought about having the two archaeologists over for dinner. A quick call to Iris and he could arrange it. But he wanted to spend the evening with Molly catching up on anything she'd discovered about the murder of Clark Partridge. He'd invite the professor over on his next trip.

"I recommend the homemade fish cakes with chili sauce and chips."

"That does sound good," Algernon said. "See you when I get back, friend." He headed toward the door, and Michael realized he was being left with the check. He had no problem with that. "Oh, and Michael, why don't you talk with your newsman Edward and any other reporters. Tell them all about Arnulph de

Mounteney and the *Seaclipse*." Michael did have a problem with that. Though he considered Edward a good reporter, he'd had his fill of newshounds.

"Lovely," he said. "Lovely. Lovely."

Michael finished his ale and called Molly. She agreed to meet him in the parking lot in about an hour. With some time on his hands, he decided a stroll around the marina would clear his head and sober him up. He might have the effects of the ale out of his system in an hour, but better to be safe and let Molly drive. He'd come back for his car tomorrow.

Hearing hammering and sawing sounds coming from one of the buildings, he thought of Rohan. He could still be working. The sun was starting to set, but there seemed no slowdown in the construction, and he knew some crews were pulling overtime. He wanted to talk to Rohan—something was niggling at him about their search for the Romanian gold. He could forge ahead on his own, but it didn't seem right to leave his Jamaican cohort out of the picture.

"Seen Rohan?" he asked one of the workers carrying boards.

"Rohan?"

"The Jamaican. Dreadlocks, beads."

"Oh, Ro!" The worker shook his head. "Ask inside. Look for Sully. He keeps track of everyone."

The store they were renovating sold boating supplies, mostly for sailboats, but they handled some light tackle for tourist-fishermen, as well, mainly an assortment of lighthouse-shaped spoon lures that said Blackpool on the side.

Sully was easy to spot. His name was embroidered in bright green letters on the pocket of his shirt.

"Is Rohan in your crew? Or is he working on Carteret's building?"

"No, he's with me…or used to be. I'm going to fire his bahookie if he doesn't show up tomorrow."

"What?"

"I said I'm going to fire his Jamaican arse if he doesn't appear."

"He didn't come in today?"

"No. And I can't call him. He doesn't have a phone. And I'm not going to waste my valuable time driving to his flat and pounding on his door. He hasn't got no flatmate, either, from what my men tell me."

"So if he's in trouble, sick or something, you wouldn't know." Michael felt a rise of anger.

"He ain't sick," Sully shot back. "If I thought he was sick, I'd send someone to check on him."

"But how can you be sure—"

"Jerry there…" Sully pointed to a young man hammering a stud in a sidewall. He was little more than a boy, likely someone pulled from a school work-study program. "Jerry saw him around lunch."

Michael headed toward Jerry.

"And don't you be keeping the boy away from his job. His time is my money," Sully called after him.

Michael held up a hand. "I'll just be a moment.

Jerry," he said in a quieter voice, "you saw Rohan today?"

"Aye, mon." He parroted the Jamaican's accent.

"What was he doing?"

"Not working here," the boy retorted. "On my break, I saw him talking to people all along the dock, asking about the shipwreck and that skeleton found not too long ago in the tunnels under the city."

A shiver passed down Michael's spine. With all the excitement about the murder, Romanian gold and the *Seaclipse,* he'd forgotten about the skeleton in the tunnels he'd stumbled across a couple of months ago.

"He's been worried about that skeleton ever since they figured out who it was."

"Huh?" Michael had thought they were still working on identifying the skeleton.

"Some old sea captain. Wortwhistle. No, wait. Chatwhistle. That was it. Alfie from the museum said it was Chatwhistle, some famous slave-ship hunter."

And maybe the sunken ship in the harbor was the one Chatwhistle had hunted, Michael thought. "But how does that have anything to do with Rohan?"

"Pardon?"

"Nothing. Sorry."

Michael scoured the docks until Molly came to get him. Rohan was nowhere to be found.

CHAPTER TWENTY

"I WAS GOING TO CALL him tonight, after dinner."

"Rohan?"

"Yeah. And thanks for coming to get me, love. I didn't really have that much to drink and walking around looking for Rohan cleared my head."

"Just what were you drinking? You smell like a pub."

"English-style—"

"Brown ale," she ventured.

"Exactly. Don't worry, it isn't likely I'll drink that stuff again for a while."

"Until the professor comes back to town," Molly said. "It's just as well that you called. They wouldn't let me in to see Percy or Dennis, and I was gearing up to make a scene."

He smiled at that image and tipped his head back. She'd put the top down on the Mini Cooper after he'd recounted what they'd seen on the dive, and he let the wind comb his hair. He listened to the radio playing. She typically didn't like the radio because she couldn't stand the commercials, or the announcer talking about a song and its artist. But tonight she had a jazz station on, though it was difficult to hear it clearly because of the wind rushing by. Still, Michael loved jazz and the music relaxed him.

The music and the wind, the company of his incredible wife, the discovery that the sunken ship was likely the *Seaclipse* and her captain, Arnulph de Mounteney—well, it was nearly a perfect day.

"I love you, Molly Graham," Michael said for no particular reason.

"And I love you, Michael Graham."

He thought her voice had a dreamy aspect. Maybe it was a good thing he couldn't find Rohan. He might have invited the Jamaican over for dinner and to work on the diorama of the town. This way, Michael could be alone with Molly.

"What's for dinner? Is Iris fixing anything? Or should we go out?"

Molly pulled a face. "We went out last night, dearest."

"Okay, what's Iris fixing?"

"Pork pies with spring onions and mushy peas."

"That sounds splendid."

Over dinner they talked about Rosamund's nonkidnapping and Molly's brief visit with her over tea.

He told her about the ship and Arnulph de Mounteney, running on so much that the mushy peas were cold by the time he got to them. They passed on dessert, which Iris said she'd freeze for Irwin, their houseman. He was away on holiday visiting with a niece and was expected back in a few days.

"And I'll have to catch him up on everything the two of you have been doing," Iris said as she cleared the plates. "Riots at the harbor, sunken ships, murder and kidnapping…well, it wasn't really a kidnapping, and the like. He'll be sorry he went to Manchester, he will."

"Ship," Michael playfully corrected. "There was only one sunken ship."

"A slaver at that," Molly said.

"Life was much less complicated before you two moved to Blackpool," Iris said, then winked. "And much less fun."

Michael and Molly took their wine to Michael's study, where he showed her the miniature buildings and the grid of Blackpool's streets. Molly looked at his handiwork, noting that some of the buildings—Rohan's—were much better made. She glanced at the rest of the room, which was a cluttered mess.

"So you're on to something, right?" Molly loomed over the diorama. "You and Rohan. Where do you think he's gone off to?"

Michael shrugged.

"I was looking for him today. Something's bugging me about these miniature buildings we put together and I wanted his input. These odd shapes…" He bent closer. "They might spell something out or connect to something. Between the outlines of the buildings and the angles of the streets…"

She peered at the models. "Sorry, I don't see it."

"For some reason I think I'm on the right track. Maybe Rohan can help with the puzzle. Though Rohan himself is a bit of a puzzle." Michael paused. "He was asking around about the shipwreck, and that one-legged skeleton found in the tunnels. Turns out that was one Captain Chatwhistle, a slave-ship hunter."

He didn't tell her that Rohan had skipped work today. "Why would he be so interested?"

She shrugged and took his empty wineglass, finding a place to set it on a bookshelf. "Would you like to dance with me, Mr. Graham? Let's forget about Rohan and the sunken ship and the murder of Clark Partridge and the kidnapping of Rosamund Carteret that wasn't a kidnapping."

"And let's forget about the harbor and the renovation and the missing chunk of grant money."

"Mmm…sounds good to me."

Michael put on an old vinyl record, a jazz classic, and took her in his arms. There wasn't much walking space in the office, so it was more like standing close and swaying to the music.

"Let's forget about everything for a little while longer," he coaxed as he escorted her from the office and down a flight to the bedroom.

CHAPTER TWENTY-ONE

MOLLY FELT DRAWN TO Blackpool's harbor today. Michael had busied himself with his diorama, so she slipped out right after breakfast, taking a thermos of tea with her in case she needed a caffeine rush to keep going.

The dredging platform was being towed away by a pair of tugboats. She fixed her gaze on the flags flying from the larger of the two tugs and blinked when it bleated its horn loudly. There were other sounds, of course, always the gulls, which some of the locals called "rats with wings." They circled the tugs, hoping to spy some tasty morsel that a crewman had dropped.

Another cloud of the birds hovered around Dennis Carteret's restaurant at the edge of the harbor. Work continued there, even though its owner remained in jail. She wondered if Rohan was working today and Michael could track him down.

Music spilled softly from a window above Barnaby's Bait Shop. Barnaby rented the upstairs out in short-term leases, and whoever was living there was playing "The Continuing Story of Bungalow Bill" from the Beatles' *White Album*. According to the renovation schedule, Barnaby's Bait Shop was scheduled for late summer with the upstairs work put off until early fall. Barnaby really shouldn't be hurt by the construction, and his business would only improve with the upgrades, she told herself. He ought to be able to command more money for upstairs flats that had plumbing and electric that met the new codes.

"What do you find so interesting about Barnaby's?" Aleister had moved so quietly Molly hadn't heard him approach. Half a head taller than she was, he looked down his nose at her, again reminding her of a vulture. "It is a quaint old building, I'll give you that. One not designed by my ancestor Charles, but certainly not one of the ugliest buildings along the wharf. I believe the renovation will be an improvement, though, don't you agree? And anything they can do to the facade will make it less of an eyesore."

Molly didn't respond, musing that the sounds of the gulls and the old Beatles tune were preferable to Aleister's nasally voice.

He swung around to stand directly in front of her, resting both his hands on the head of his cane. "Pity the dredging had to stop."

Are you trying to pick a fight? Molly wondered. *Or at the very least you're hoping to publicly upset me.* She noticed a few shopkeepers were watching her and Crowe. *Smarmy* was a word her mother used to use. It applied perfectly to Aleister.

"It is a pity," she replied, "but it'll start again…after the archaeologists and the historians are done with the sunken ship."

Did Aleister flinch? Had she seen right?

"Perhaps," he said. He leaned back on his heels a moment, plucking the cane up and holding it in front of him now, parallel to the ground. "Unless the grant money runs out before then. Do tell me, Molly, any word on how old Carteret is going to repay what he stole?"

At that moment Molly believed Aleister could indeed have perpetrated the fake kidnapping. Aleister Crowe was more than capable of pulling his brother's strings—or Clark Partridge's—and getting either one of them to call Dennis and claim to have kidnapped Rosamund. Aleister wouldn't have sullied his hands by killing Partridge himself—of that she was certain. But he had enough money that he could have hired it done. But what was he so intent on hiding? What secret would have caused him to go to such lengths?

Aleister had said something else, but she'd missed it, caught up in her own thoughts. She stepped to his right to get around him, bumping her thermos against his leg.

"Oh, excuse me," she said.

"Planning to make a day of it out here?" He gestured with his chin at the thermos.

"Perhaps."

"No doubt you want to watch the construction

crews. See how that grant money you got the town is being spent."

She let out a hissing breath and clicked her heels together. "Aleister, it's none of your business what I'm doing out here." Molly instantly regretted the words. She might have been thinking them, but she hadn't meant to say them out loud.

"You're angry with me," he said flatly. "I've done something to upset you and—"

"Aleister, I'm just…busy…and—"

"Is it the August Historical Preservation Society?"

"What?"

"The society? And Miss Coffey? I've been speaking to her about the new building codes, and—"

"Aleister, you've caused a rift between me and the society. I don't appreciate or need that. But I'm not on the planning board. Maybe I should take an advertisement out in the *Blackpool Journal* that says 'Molly Graham is not on the planning board. All Molly Graham did was get this town a damnable green grant. Molly Graham meant well, and didn't mean to stir up some hornet's nest.'" She felt the red rising in her face and her stomach churning.

Maybe she did have an ulcer, one the size of Blackpool's harbor. Why had she come out here today? To watch the construction? To run into the brick wall that was Aleister Crowe? She suddenly wished that Crowe did have a hand in the fake kidnapping and that the

D.C.I. would get some evidence on him and lock him up for a long time.

"I've decided, or rather Aubrey's decided, to close the building in question." Aleister spoke calmly, as if Molly hadn't launched a verbal tirade at him. "There's a tavern on the first floor, and a few flats on the second, storage on the third. To avoid smacking heads with the planning board, and rather than make one more useless appeal to you, the building will be shut up. I've checked the board's new codes. If a building is not open to the public, it does not have to meet the new codes."

Molly groaned and walked away, heading toward Dennis's restaurant. She'd just decided she wanted to observe the construction work.

She reached her free hand into her pocket and pulled out her iPhone, touching the button that called Michael. "Want to join me for a second breakfast?" she asked. "I can smell the bangers. I just walked by that little café you like."

"See you in a bit."

CHAPTER TWENTY-TWO

MICHAEL HAD MOVED some of the model buildings around—busywork, really, something to keep his hands occupied while his mind churned over the past several days' events.

He was glad when Molly called and mentioned a second breakfast. The little he'd eaten early hadn't been enough, and he wanted to talk to her more about the fake kidnapping.

Besides, maybe he might run in to Rohan down by the docks.

He pulled into a parking spot several blocks from the water, thankful he'd found one this close. It was a small lot full of local cars and rent-a-cars from the tourists, and there was a stunted tour bus pulling away, filled with what looked like senior citizens. There was a news van, and he saw Jennessee hovering around it. That meant her cameraman was nearby, and probably the chap from the BBC, too.

He got out of the car and thrust the keys deep in his pocket, finding a piece of balsa wood from his diorama work. He struck out toward the harbor.

Aleister and Aubrey stood at the edge of the main

dock, the older Crowe gesturing out to sea and the dredging platform, the back of which was disappearing from view around the bend. He knew Molly wouldn't be anywhere near the Crowes, so he scanned the rest of the crowd. The weather was pleasant and the docks served as a magnet, drawing locals and visitors. Reporters were around because of the ship, and construction workers…and Gypsies.

Throughout the country Gypsies were rarely welcomed into an area. The locals frowned on them for parking caravans in vacant lots or at the edge of a town, canvassing down each block and offering to do tree cutting or lawn weeding, then traveling along to the next burg, leaving suspicion in their wake. The Draghicis hadn't seemed to be looking for any sort of work, Michael thought. But they were no doubt looking for gold.

Speak of the devil, Michael thought. Stefan Draghici was headed straight for him, Esma in tow.

"Michael Graham, I have wanted to speak with you." Stefan's voice was thickly Romanic today, and Michael knew it was put on; he'd heard the man talk many times before with barely any accent. "You have not returned my phone calls."

"I don't believe I've returned any phone calls in the past few days," Michael admitted. He shook the hand Stefan extended, noticing it was calloused. "I've been busy."

"Busy with something that does not concern you."

Stefan dropped Michael's hand and set his fists against his waist in a pose that reminded Michael of Johnny Depp playing Captain Jack Sparrow. Dressed so colorfully and with his long hair, he could well play the part.

"I'm sorry, I don't—"

"My gold. My gold should not concern you."

"What makes you think—"

"That it is *my* gold? I have told the newsmen this, and Esma has told your wife. It is common knowledge that Charles Crowe swindled my ancestors and stole their gold. By rights it belongs to us."

"Why do you assume I have it?"

"I know you do not," Stefan replied sharply. "But you search for it. At the library you go over maps. At the museum of ships, you go over maps. One man says you have built a town in your home and that you study it late into the evening. This man, he says that you are obsessed with the treasure hunt."

Rohan? Had Rohan talked to Stefan? And if so, why?

"England is a free country," Michael replied.

"I will warn you one more time—stop your hunt."

"I can't be the only one looking." Michael noticed that his exchange with Stefan had drawn the attention of a few passersby. They hovered within earshot, pretending to be admiring the sailboats. "If the gold is here—and some people say it's all a fable—others are searching, too."

"But you," Stefan returned almost angrily. "You have resources and nothing else to do except pursue what belongs to me." The veins in his neck stood out and his eyes glistened. "If you are a respectable, good man, you will give me all the clues you have unearthed about the gold."

"Nothing," Michael said flatly. "So far I've come up with nothing." Stefan looked like a volcano ready to erupt. Michael glanced around frantically, hoping to see Molly. "Stefan, why don't you spend your time searching for the gold yourself rather than—"

"Bothering you? Tell me, Michael Graham, do you know anything about my family? If you did, you would realize we deserve this gold."

"To be honest, Stefan, I don't—"

"My family, it traces its roots to Pakistan, from the Rom tribe. We left India and traveled to Armenia and Persia. So old is my family that there is record of my ancestors in the Byzantine Empire after the days of the Seljuk Turk attacks. We moved into the Balkans, to Wallachia and Moldavia, before the land fell to the Ottomans. Some members of our clan to this day can be found near these migration paths. I have traveled it myself and—"

"This is all very interesting, but—"

"When the Draghicis came into Europe in the west we carried letters from the Hungarian king that should have afforded us protection and privilege. But the people of Europe do not like our way of life and persecuted us. My ancestors had no word for possession, Michael Graham, for 'owning' a thing as you Europeans do. In Europe, property is sacrosanct— sacred. And so you call us thieves because we take things to survive. Yet Charles Crowe was the real thief. He stole Draghici gold."

Michael would have been more sympathetic to Stefan's story had the clan leader not slipped into and out of his thick Romanian accent. Still, he listened as the man continued.

"My ancestors came to Romania to make a better life for their children, and ended up being the slaves of landowners. We were freed in 1851, but still we struggled. I have relatives in Romania so poor they pull carts along the road, not able to afford a motor car. They live on little pieces of land where villages end. The gold would make a difference to us." Stefan took a step back and puffed out his chest. "You do not need the money, Michael Graham. You and your American wife have more than enough. You do not need to be searching for Draghici coins."

Esma shook a finger at Michael for good measure. "My husband, he has not threatened you. But I...I will curse you and any offspring you conceive if you do not stop your pursuit of our gold. I will go to any lengths to regain what is rightfully ours. I will do anything—"

Anything? Pretend to kidnap Rosamund Carteret and then kill Clark Partridge?

Could Esma be capable of such acts? It would net them one hundred and fifty thousand pounds. The gold would be worth more than that, likely, but one hundred and fifty thousand pounds was not something to sneeze at.

Esma continued to wag her finger. "My husband, he will not threaten you, Michael Graham. But I am not so civil!"

The couple turned and would have melted into the crowd on the docks if not for their colorful clothes and exaggerated swagger.

Michael watched them go. In truth, he didn't care about the treasure. But he needed the hunt and the puzzle, the game of it. He wouldn't stop his search just because the Draghicis considered him their only competition for the loot. A thought flickered at the edge of his mind, that maybe he should join forces with Stefan and help the Gypsies find the gold. But first he'd confirm that the coins really did belong to their ancestors.

If they even existed.

Now, about that second breakfast… Michael pivoted and headed toward the café, thinking Molly might already be there waiting for him. He abruptly ran into a line of protestors who'd spilled onto the docks. No wonder Molly was so flummoxed by the rabble around here. Oh, for a quiet week at Thorne-Shower Manor.

"Go Green!" one of them hollered.

"Green is victory!" shouted a girl in a Green Gladiators T-shirt, her hair such a mass of tangles that he almost expected a bird to fly out of it.

Michael stopped and watched them march past.

"Victory is ours!" croaked an elderly woman wearing emerald-green pants and an olive-green blouse with flouncy ruffles at the sleeves. To Michael she could have passed for a large leprechaun.

"Victory!" A chant began, drowning out the music and the beggar gulls and punctured by a tugboat bleat.

"Victory is sweet." This came from Weymouth, who appeared at Michael's shoulder. "Too bad Molly isn't here for me to gloat."

Michael whirled to face him, but the other man kept speaking.

"I would like to tell your wife how glad I am that some of that grant money was stolen. It's unfortunate that the entire fund was not taken."

Michael opened his mouth for an angry retort, but Weymouth wasn't finished.

"I would gloat to her about the theft and hail Dennis Carteret as a hero to the environment. Work has slowed—"

"Do you hear that?" Michael shot back. "That hammering? The sound of a band saw? I don't think the renovations have been delayed."

"But the dredging crew is gone," Weymouth said.

He was positively leering. "The harbor is safe. I could give a rat's ass what they do to the buildings, provided they don't dump their garbage into the bay. The dredging, now that was the real—"

"But the dredgers will be back," Michael said. He was instantly sorry he'd engaged the Green Gladiator in conversation. And yet he pressed on. "When the matter with the *Seaclipse*—"

"So that's the name of the sunken ship."

"When the matter with the *Seaclipse* is resolved, the dredging will continue."

Weymouth shook his head. "That will take a while, and it will give us plenty of time to come up with counterstudies to show just how damaging the dredging will be to marine life."

Michael didn't bother to hide his ire. "Don't you get it? Don't you read anything? There's too much silt in the harbor. And chemicals discharged from chemical plants that operate to the north of us. Dredging will help get rid of them. It will make things *better* for the marine life."

"The planning board made their studies say exactly what they wanted them to say. They wanted the harbor deeper for larger boats so they could bring more money into Blackpool. Our studies will reveal the truth."

"You mean they'll show what *you* want them to show." Michael glared at Weymouth. "You're so narrow-minded, Francis. You can't see the big picture because all you have in the wallet of your mind is this tiny snapshot. You and your misguided fellows—"

A scream and a splash stopped the men's argument. It was followed by a constable's shrill whistle and shouts. Weymouth took off running toward the commotion and Michael darted for the café, watching the ruckus as he went.

Apparently the Green Gladiators were clashing with the Draghicis, and it looked to Michael like some of the construction workers were trying to break up a fight. He didn't see any dreadlocks and beads in the mix, though he hoped Rohan was in the vicinity and had returned to work. He'd look for Rohan after a good meal with Molly—once things had settled down.

The constable—Sergeant Krebs probably, since he'd spotted her several minutes before—continued to tweet away.

"Green is victory!"

Michael closed the café door behind him and spotted Molly at a table in the center, a mug of tea held up to her nose.

The waitress presented menus before he sat down.

"I'll have the special," he told her. "Uh…what is the special today?"

"Rashers of crisp bacon, two bangers, field mushrooms sautéed in butter, two fried eggs, tomatoes and baked beans in tomato sauce."

"Fine. I'll have that with some Henderson's relish, and some toast and marmalade."

"Porridge oats and a grapefruit for me," Molly said. "And a refill on the tea."

"Tea for me, too," Michael said. "And one of your Bloody Marys."

Molly raised an eyebrow.

"Forget the bloody Bloody Mary," he said. "Just tea."

"Hungry today?" Molly asked.

"I'm something today," he mumbled. Michael proceeded to tell her about his encounters on the docks, took a breath and listened while she told him about her run-in with the Crowe brothers.

"And to think Blackpool is touted as a pleasant, sleepy town," Michael grumbled.

"It is most of the time."

"When people aren't killing each other."

"There's a strong possibility that Aleister could be behind these protests—maybe even the fake kidnapping and the murder of Clark Partridge, too."

Michael accepted the cup of tea the waitress brought. "I think it's more likely Francis Weymouth is the culprit. He's incited the Green Gladiators. There are more of them out there today than when they descended during the groundbreaking. He's smart and scheming, and he could have concocted the whole ransom scheme as a way to drain money from the harbor. As for killing Clark Partridge…well, maybe it was an accident. Or maybe he murdered Partridge just to shut him up."

It was her turn to disagree. "First, I don't believe

someone accidentally cut Partridge's throat. And as for shutting him up, Partridge had a record. He wouldn't have run to the authorities. So who would have needed to silence him? Second, Weymouth might go to extremes in the name of the environment, or what he perceives to be an ecological cause, but the more I think about it, the less likely it seems he's involved. As you said, he's smart. There are lots of ways for protestors to hold up a project. Weymouth didn't need to orchestrate something so complex—not to mention illegal and immoral."

Michael finished his first cup of tea as the waitress came with their order.

"That was fast," he said.

"It's the special. It's always on the stove."

Molly spooned some brown sugar into her porridge.

"So, not Weymouth," Michael agreed. His words were muffled, his mouth full of eggs that were a little on the runny side. "But I'm skeptical that Aleister would stoop to something like this."

"So who else?" Molly dug into the porridge and pronounced it delicious.

"Esma."

"Esma?"

"Yeah, she gives me the shivers." Michael speared one of the bangers. "You know, she had the gall to curse me! I was actually considering helping Stefan find the gold. I think he really might have a legitimate claim to it. Besides, it would frost the cupcakes of some of these bigoted locals if the Draghicis won the treasure."

"You told Stefan that?"

"No. Not yet. Curious, but he may have been talking to Rohan. When I'm done here I'm going to stroll down the wharf and see—"

"Rohan didn't go to work today," Molly interrupted. "I checked before coming in here. And he doesn't need to bother about showing up tomorrow. He's been fired."

"Then where in the bloody blue blazes *is* Rohan?"

"The better questions, Michael, are just how well do you know him, and what is he capable of?"

"I'm not so sure anymore…."

CHAPTER TWENTY-THREE

"IF YOU DON'T MIND, Molly, I'm going in search of Rohan. Stop by his flat, talk to some of the neighbors."

"I don't mind at all."

"I'm just a little worried about him."

"Because he's been talking to Stefan Draghici and asking about one-legged skeletons and sunken ships?"

"Because maybe—just maybe—what if he has something to do with Partridge's death? He has been acting strangely lately." He pushed away his empty plate. "But, I hope that's not the case. He is my friend, and I'm going to find him."

"And I…" Molly stood and brushed at a spot on her blouse where the grapefruit had squirted her. "I am going home. I am going to curl up in the most comfortable chair we have—"

"That would be the overstuffed wing-backed one I helped you drag into the study."

"And read that Lillian Stewart Carl book on the top of my stack. It's time I read a good mystery and took a break from trying to solve one."

"A capital idea, Mrs. Graham. But it's all talk. I know you won't let this mystery drop because I can't, either. So you think about that mystery book, and give me a call on my mobile to let me know where you really are. We'll meet up later and compare notes." He put several euros on the table to cover the bill and the tip, then took her hand and escorted her from the café.

The ruckus had died down, and there were four constables on the scene. Sergeant Krebs was leading Stefan away in handcuffs. Esma followed and scolded the constable with each step.

Another constable, the one Michael had seen doing crosswords on the dredging platform, led away a thoroughly soaked Green Gladiator. Jennessee Stanwood and her cameraman walked behind, recording the events for the evening news.

When the entourage had passed, Michael drew Molly in close and kissed her. "Weeks from now this might be a sleepy little town again," he said.

"You wish."

"See you later." He scampered off.

"Later," Molly said, angling toward the other end of the lot and crossing paths with Aleister again. She felt the porridge churning in her stomach.

"Did you enjoy breakfast, Mrs. Graham?"

Molly decided not to answer and tried to step around him.

"Did you and Michael discuss the latest news over tea?"

That comment got her to stop. She turned to face him, fixing her gaze on the silver crow atop his walking stick.

"Just what is the latest news, Aleister?" She braced herself for something that would probably make her stomach churn faster.

"Oh, you didn't hear? And I thought you got on so well with the D.C.I. I thought you were friends."

"Aleister—"

"D.C.I. Paddington has arrested someone for the murder of that unfortunate man, young Clark Partridge. He's no doubt the one who instigated that heinous false kidnapping scheme, too." Aleister thumped the end of his cane against the ground. "I'm surprised the D.C.I. didn't call you." He raised the cane and looked down it, as if he were sighting her. "But then, maybe you and he aren't friends after all."

Molly decided the Lillian Stewart Carl book would have to wait. She walked deliberately to her car and drove downtown to the police station.

CHAPTER TWENTY-FOUR

A YELLOW CAR WAS PARKED across the street from the police station, right in front of the jail. Molly pulled behind it, put the top up and got out just as Rosamund emerged from the jail, a large paper sack clutched in front of her.

"Rosamund!"

"Hi...Molly, isn't it?"

"Yes, Molly Graham."

"Are you here to visit my father? He'd enjoy the company. I didn't stay as long as he would have liked." She shivered and pulled a face. "That place creeps me out, about as much as being on my billy tod in that big old house."

Molly had to think a moment. She was pretty adept at understanding British slang, but she hadn't heard that one before. "Billy tod?"

"Billy tod—you know, all alone. On my own. A big, creaky house all by myself."

Molly smiled. "Billy tod. I'll have to remember that."

"So, are you going to see my father and Percy?"

"Yes, I will, but I've got business at the police station first."

Rosamund pulled an even more exaggerated face. "Well, when you get around to chatting with Dad, tell him to calm down."

"Calm—"

"He's got his knickers all in a twist 'cause I'm taking another holiday. He thinks I've got it in my head to do something naughty. I don't have a boyfriend, though I wouldn't be opposed to one. I just have to get out of here for a few days. All the phone calls. I can't go anywhere in town that people aren't on me about my father. Either it's some local who wants to tell me how rotten it was that Dad stole the city's money or some old fart wants to be all sympathetic and bring me a pie and pat my hand, saying 'there, there, it'll be all right.' It's not going to be all right. Dad's locked up and probably is going to do prison time. It's not like I give a duck what the people around here think, but they won't let it be. And they won't let *me* be. God, the phone keeps ringing. I'm just tired of it. I need to get away."

"I understand." Molly really did. She felt like she wanted to get away from it all, too. "Where are you going?"

"Back to London, but just for a handful of days. I've some friends there I can stay with."

Molly wanted to say, "This time tell your dad exactly where you are." But she bit her tongue. It wasn't her business or her place, and it wasn't as if Carteret could call out to check on the girl. Instead, she said, "Just stay in touch with your father. You're his world, Rosamund. He's in jail because—"

"I *know*. He's in jail because he's a soft old coot who fell for some scheme."

Molly wanted to reach out and hug the girl, but she stayed at arm's length.

Rosamund clutched the sack tighter, the paper making a crinkly sound. "At least they let him wear his own clothes. Percy, he's stuck with jail issue. His wife is angry and isn't bringing him anything from home." She smiled at that. "Dad gave me this shirt to take home and wash. They'd put some piss-artist in with him who barfed all over." She shuddered again and wrinkled her nose. "Any road, hopefully Dad's not going to be in that stinking cell for too much longer. Barrister says there'll be a hearing, and he'll try to get Dad released and under…"

"House arrest?"

"Something like that. But after the trial they'll probably lock him up in some big prison for a time."

"I'm sorry, Rosamund." Molly sincerely meant it. "You're going to be away just for a few days on this holiday, right?"

"To clear my head. I wouldn't call it much of a holiday, though. I mean, I'm not going off to have a giggle with some lad." She rolled her eyes and nodded at her car. "I gotta run and throw this and some other things in the wash."

Molly watched her drive away and then crossed the street to the police station. She'd talk to Dennis when she was done with Paddington, if they'd let her. Maybe, just maybe, she'd be able to relate some good news: that D.C.I. Paddington had caught the man who had caused all this trouble.

The station was a whir of activity. Three constables were at desks banging away on computer keyboards, probably working on reports. Two assistants bustled back and forth between printers and the desks, one nearly bumping into Molly as she made her way toward Paddington's office.

"Can I help you?" The woman stopped in front of Molly. The other assistant disappeared down the hall with a stack of papers.

"I'm here to see D.C.I. Paddington."

"Did you check in at the desk?"

"No, not yet." Molly walked back to the front desk. She recognized the elderly woman behind it.

"Do you have an appointment, flower?"

"No, I don't."

"I think you'll have to call later. He's—"

"Very busy, I'm sure. Everyone looks busy."

"There's a lot going on today, Mrs. Graham."

"I just want to talk to him for a few minutes. I have some ideas—"

The front door banged open and Sergeant Krebs

tromped in. "Cor blimey!" Krebs said, tugging off her hat and wiping at the sweat on her forehead. Molly turned her attention to the sergeant. Krebs rested her back against the door.

"Something wrong?" asked one of the constables. Molly noticed he didn't look up.

"Damn long day it's been already. This harbor duty is like…is like…well, it's bloody smeggy. It's awful." Krebs took stock of Molly and grimaced. "The Green Gladiators were celebrating, the lot of them whooping it up about the stolen money and the dredgers leaving. The Gypsies got in the way of the party, I guess. And then some salad dodger on the construction crew stuck his gut in the way trying to make peace. Make pieces is what they all ended up doing to each other. One of the Gladiators landed up in the harbor, pushed by a Draghici, and ended up in the backseat of Williams's car. I wasn't going to arrest him. I figured I had seniority over Williams. Let him sop up after the lout."

"I thought you wanted harbor duty." The constable still didn't look up. "On the board, you requested it."

"I took the king Gypsy," Krebs said. "And he was none too happy about it. I charged him with disorderly. Hell, I could've charged the lot of them with disorderly—every single soul down on the docks."

"You've been racking up the disorderlies," the constable said. He finally looked up and waved a pencil at Krebs. "Quite the tally for the week."

"Yeah, well, I could've had more."

"Jail's not big enough," the assistant observed. "Not for all the rabble-rousers down at the docks."

Krebs stared, and Molly got the sense that the sergeant was measuring her. "Of course, we wouldn't have to throw any of them in jail if they weren't so riled up over everything."

"The Gypsies don't care about the harbor." Molly surprised herself by commenting.

"I know," Krebs said. "They're just after the gold. But if it exists, they aren't going to find it down by the docks. And that shipwreck…I heard it was a slaver."

Krebs pushed off from the door and tromped to the water cooler, taking a long drink and wiping at her face again. "So why do you want to talk to the D.C.I.?"

"I already told her the D.C.I. is busy," the assistant called.

"I understand he's arrested someone for the murder of Clark Partridge," Molly said. "I was the one who found Partridge's body the other day and—"

Krebs shook her head. "He's still questioning a pair of Partridge's friends. Round two of it. One of 'em's a real speed freak we've taken for drugs on more than one occasion."

"Two?"

"Two sods, and I figure either one's good for it."

Krebs seemed to consider for a moment, then said, "Come with me. I can't guarantee you'll get to talk to the D.C.I., but you can get a look at him and the suspects."

Molly raised an eyebrow in surprise.

They were in a narrow hall leading to the back of the Victorian, and Krebs gestured to the first door on the right. "The D.C.I. is talking to them in there. But we can have a look-see from in here." She went to the next door, opened it and gestured for Molly to enter first.

"Thank you for this," Molly said, perplexed at why Krebs was being so cordial. She'd only seen the sergeant act rough-and-tumble before. Maybe she had a softer side.

"I figure this is the least I can do," Krebs said. She pointed to a bench in front of a picture window set into the wall.

Molly realized she was looking through a two-way mirror into what amounted to be the interrogation room. Krebs took a seat on the bench and patted it. Molly sat next to her. This close, she couldn't help but smell Krebs. There was a touch of salt from being by the harbor, and sweat from exertion, but under that she smelled something familiar: Bvlgari Pour Femme, a perfume that was on her own dresser. Slightly floral, its ingredients included jasmine tea, pepper and rose, and cost about 600 euros an ounce.

"Just like the *Law and Order* television show," Krebs said. "We can hear them." She leaned forward and flicked a switch. "But they can't hear us. The one on the right is Nigel Loftus. The other is Nick Atkinson, a sometimes-partner of Partridge and a real Herbert, always getting busted for speed and hot-kniving pot. But then, you met Nick, didn't you? I saw you and your husband at his flat when we were pulling up."

"Actually, Michael called you about Mr. Atkinson."

Krebs rolled her shoulders.

"Thanks," Molly said again. "For this."

"I should be the one thanking you. Like I said, this is the least I can do. What with all the uproar in the marina, and the arrests I've made—none of which would have happened without you and that grant—I'm bound to get a promotion."

CHAPTER TWENTY-FIVE

THE TWO SUSPECTS WERE SEATED at a metal table. One half of the tabletop was covered with Formica, the other had been picked off over the years. There was writing all over it, racial slurs, stick figure drawings and various uncomplimentary names for the police. From her vantage point, Molly couldn't make out all of the scrawls.

Paddington paced in front of the table, close to the two-way mirror, sweat circles dark under his arms, his shirt rumpled. His heels clicked rhythmically and were the only sounds Molly heard through the small speaker.

"He's using the old silent tactic on them," Krebs explained.

When Molly didn't say anything, the sergeant continued, coming across like a school teacher lecturing a thick student.

"The silence unnerves crooks, rattles their cages and makes them talk. They hate the silence."

Paddington continued to pace. Even Molly was getting unnerved by the silence from the other room. Couldn't someone in there say something?

Just that instant her cell sounded from inside her pocket, Pachelbel's Canon signaling that Michael was calling. She reached in and turned off the iPhone. She'd call him later.

Paddington stopped in front of the table and bent forward, arms spread wide and fingers splayed. His back was to her, but Molly could well imagine the determined expression that must be etched on his face, all the little wrinkles around his eyes helping to make him look fierce.

Still, he said nothing.

Krebs leaned back and smiled. "One of 'em will start talking now, just you watch."

Molly whispered, concerned that somehow her voice might carry into the interrogation room. "Do you know much about them?"

Krebs did nothing to mute her voice. "I know that neither one of them has made a request for a barrister. That means they are cocky, broke or innocent and don't think they need one. I vote for cocky or broke. Those two aren't the innocent type."

Molly kept her voice low. "This Nick, you said he's—"

"He was," Kreb corrected, "a friend of Clark Partridge. Probably the dead bloke's closest friend. They were flatmates on and off for the past few years at least."

Molly craned her neck to get a better look at Atkinson. He was as disheveled as he'd been when she and

Michael had talked to him at his flat. Late twenties, but maybe younger. The drug use had added a few years at least.

"See that scar on his cheek? The one that disappears in the beard he's trying to grow?"

Molly nodded.

"He got that about a year and a half ago when he and Partridge were drunk and got into a fight over some bet they'd placed on a game of footy. Partridge hit him with a broken beer bottle. Partridge felt bad enough to cover the hospital bill…no idea where he got the money. Probably sold some drugs."

Atkinson looked…*dirty* was the only word Molly could come up with. His face was smudged with grime, his T-shirt was worn at the collar and there was a stain straight down from his chin. She'd gotten a glimpse of his pants before Paddington had stopped in front of the table. They were faded jeans and sliced at the knees, probably a deliberate fashion statement. His shoes were old sandals with tire treads for soles.

"His record shows several instances of fights," Krebs continued, "though nothing major. He's never put anyone in the hospital for longer than it takes them to get a gash stitched up. But he gets violent when he's cornered."

"And the other gentleman?" she whispered.

"Gentleman?" This time Krebs whispered back to poke fun at her. "That would be the Nigel Loftus I mentioned." She raised her voice again. "A bookie,

smuggler. You name it. If it's illegal and there's dosh attached, Nigel will give it a go."

"A smuggler." Molly thought it might not be much of a stretch for someone like that to add kidnapping to his repertoire, even if it was a fake kidnapping.

"The D.C.I. caught him three years ago—that was before I started here, but it's in his records. Trying to take some old artifact out of the Maritime Museum. So add thief to his list. But he didn't get out the door with it. Old Alfie should have let him leave the premises. Then he would have done more time. I think he got three months, which, as they say, he could do standing on his head."

Molly could tell the man was older than Atkinson, probably closer to Michael's age. His visage was chiseled and hard-edged, like a statue, and his shaved head gleamed in the fluorescent light. He had tattoos. A hawk's or eagle's head rose out of his shirt collar and stopped halfway up his neck. Images of barbed wire circled both forearms. There was another tattoo on the side of his head, an octopus or squid, or some fantastical beast with tentacles. She couldn't see it clearly... and didn't want to. The man gave her the willies. Despite his outwardly nasty appearance, he was slight, and his nose was so long that he reminded Molly of a rabid ferret. The look was completed with a bright crimson soul patch.

"I'd say he's probably Blackpool's most notorious git," Krebs said.

"I've been doing a lot of thinking," Molly admitted, "trying to come up with who could have claimed to kidnap Rosamund Carteret, and who might have been capable of murdering Partridge. I was focusing on the renovation and the dredging, assuming that the kidnapping and murder were somehow connected."

"I don't think Atkinson or Loftus give a rat's arse about the harbor. They care about money."

"Did they find it?" Molly had raised her voice a little, finally realizing they couldn't be heard in the interrogation room.

"Find what?"

"The hundred and fifty thousand pounds. Any trace of it?"

"Not in either man's flat," Krebs said. "Not in Partridge's room, either. But that doesn't mean they don't have it in some hidey-hole. Sods like them would have places to stash it."

Paddington still hadn't said anything. Molly looked at her watch and considered calling Michael back if this "silent treatment" was going to last much longer.

"I told you an hour ago I don't know nothing about Party's murder." This came from Atkinson. "I ain't seen Party for a week or so. What else do you want me to say?"

Molly realized Party was Atkinson's nickname for Partridge. She remembered someone else calling him that, too....

"Told you," Krebs said. "If you stay quiet long enough, the perps talk. They can't stand the silence."

Paddington started pacing again.

"And I don't know this bloke." Atkinson gestured with his head at Loftus. His fingers picked faster at the Formica. Molly saw that his thumb was bloody—he might have ripped his nail on the table. "Well, I know *who* he is, but that's about it."

Paddington stood behind the men now, leaning forward and glancing from one to the other before resuming his pacing.

"All right," Atkinson continued. "I might have done business with ol' Nigel once or twice."

Nigel's ferret eyes narrowed and his lip curled at that.

"Maybe twice."

Paddington slowed his steps and stopped in front of the table again.

"Party did business with Nigel, though. You should be asking Nigel about Party."

"I asked both of you the same questions." It was the first time Molly had heard Paddington speak to the men. "That was more than an hour ago."

"Well, I'll tell you the same thing that I told you an hour ago. I didn't ice Party. He was my mate. Since we were tykes. I wouldn't ice Party. I wouldn't ice anybody." He paused. "Don't you get it? I'm trying to be a better person."

Krebs laughed.

"I'm trying to mend my ways. I even go to church now and again."

"You shared a flat with Partridge." The D.C.I. stood directly in front of Atkinson now so Molly couldn't see him.

"Yeah, he was my flatmate. A while ago. Not recently."

"And you said you hadn't seen him in a…how did you put it…a week or so."

"I'm not his minder. He goes…went off on his own from time to time."

The room fell silent again, and Molly reached for her mobile. Krebs leaned over.

"You can tell that the D.C.I. doesn't think Atkinson did it. Oh, he was a possibility, but he's just been eliminated from the D.C.I.'s short list."

To Molly it looked like the D.C.I. was hitting Atkinson up for it pretty hard.

"Why?"

"He was betting hard on Loftus from the start. One, he's got ties to Partridge. Two, Loftus and Partridge used to be mates, but word on the street is that something soured between them recently. Three, and this is the damning one, Loftus has been linked to three other murders outside Blackpool, and no one—not even the D.C.I.—has been able to get enough evidence to arrest him."

Loftus finally said something.

"What was that?" Paddington demanded. "I didn't hear you."

"I said you're looking in the wrong place." The sneer on Loftus's face gave Molly goose bumps.

"You had a falling out with Clark Partridge."

"That's no secret."

"Then tell me why I shouldn't charge you with his murder?"

Loftus made a growling sound from deep in his throat and spat out a gob of phlegm. "Partridge owed me money. Being mates only goes so far. He owed me five thousand, and that was before interest. Why would I kill him? Alive, I had a chance to get my money back."

"Why did he owe you money?"

Loftus sighed. "Party liked to gamble—he'd run up a big debt."

Paddington straightened and folded his arms. "So who came up with the kidnapping scheme, you or Partridge? Which one of you saw it as a way to erase Partridge's debt? Did Partridge think he could repay you and set up a sizeable nest egg on top of that? Did you cooperate and then kill him so you could keep all of the money? You've got a reputation for violence, Mr. Loftus."

Loftus chortled. "I have an alibi, and you have no motive. If you did, you'd arrest me. I'd not be sitting here."

"Maybe I will arrest you. And maybe you do have

an alibi, flimsy as it is. But at minimum I have you on taking illegal gambling bets. Minimum. I've no problem with locking you up 'til you sprout age spots."

Loftus grew a shade paler. "Look. Party was a sometimes-friend, and yes, Party owed me money. But he promised me he was going to pay me back soon. He had some scheme up his sleeve, something he was involved in that would yield a good chunk of dosh. I didn't ask him the particulars because he also said he wasn't keen on the plan, and that he hoped he could come up with another way to pay me back. I just told him he'd better make it quick."

Paddington turned back to Atkinson. "Your mate Loftus here claims he wasn't involved in the kidnapping ploy. But Partridge did have an accomplice. Partridge wasn't smart enough to hatch the scheme on his own. But you…I think you were smart enough."

"I done told you again and again. I got nothing to do with Party's death. And I didn't know nothing about any kidnapping and ransom, and I sure as hell didn't know about any hundred and fifty thousand pounds… or I would've had me some of it."

"I can find a reason to charge you for something more than the drug possession I've already got you on," Paddington said. "Lock you away for a very long time."

"Honest. I hadn't seen Party in at least a week. He'd gotten himself some girlfriend, and he was shacking up with her. I was surprised to learn Party was dead.

I didn't think he was back in town. I figured he was still holidaying."

A memory clicked in Molly's mind. She jumped up and burst into the interrogation room.

"I know who killed Partridge!" she shouted. "I know who staged the kidnapping and who has the money. C'mon, we have to hurry!"

CHAPTER TWENTY-SIX

SHE REACHED FOR her mobile and turned it back on as she quickly brought Paddington up to speed. As soon as they stepped out of the station, she shot ahead of Paddington toward her car. "I'll meet you there!"

"You'll do no such thing," he hollered.

She stopped in her tracks. "But I figured it out!"

"Molly Graham, if you're going over there, you're going *with* me. Now, hurry it up." He ran for his car and she jogged along to catch up. Pachelbel's Canon played as she went, then it shifted to voice mail. She slipped into the front seat next to the D.C.I. and pulled on her seat belt. Her mobile rang again, "Eleanor Rigby" this time. She fished it out and looked at the tiny screen. It was Arliss.

Molly would get back to her, and to Michael. As Paddington drove away from the curb she saw that she had eight voice-mail messages waiting, calls her mobile had collected while she watched the interview in the police station.

Paddington picked up his radio. "Marge, have Sergeant Krebs arrest Loftus on an illegal gambling charge and add him to the collection of souls at the jail. You can release Atkinson, but make him squirm a little first. Actually, have Krebs do that, too. She's good at making people squirm."

Molly glanced at the eight messages: five from Michael, one from Arliss, one from Aleister—how did he get her number?—and one from Edward, the reporter. She dialed Michael's mobile, speaking softly so not to disturb Paddington.

"Michael, what's so important that you keep calling me?"

"Molly! Where are you?"

"Where am I? I'm in Paddington's car. And no, I haven't been arrested. We're going to arrest someone. I'll tell you about it later. I'm going to turn off my mobile again for a while—"

"Okay. I thought you'd want to hear—those other grants came through."

"What? Really?" Her voice rose and her words came faster. "Why, that's wonderful! And that's why Arliss was calling, no doubt. Aleister and Edward, too. Oh, Michael, this should get Barnaby and Clement to sit back and shut up. Thanks for letting me know."

"Wait, who are you going to arrest?"

"I'll tell you about the murderer later. I'll call you back."

She turned off the iPhone and stuck it in her pocket.

Blackpool's streets were narrow, and Paddington navigated them quickly, but without the siren. Molly knew he didn't want to alert the murderer that he was coming. His car radio crackled with reports from another constable, and he switched it off.

"That was Michael," Molly said.

"I gathered." Paddington kept his eyes on the street and nearly struck a car as he barreled through the intersection. The newer streets on the inland side of town were wider, but the ones in the heart of the city and near the harbor were painfully narrow, many of them still boasting the original cobblestones. They'd been intended for carriages and wagons "back in the day," when there wasn't a need for two lanes to accommodate motor traffic.

"Blackpool is going to get another seven hundred thousand pounds in grant money. That'll just about cover all the historical work. Barnaby and Clement won't have to shell out much, if any, of their own money. Their objections to the work…well, they'll have nothing to object to. They'll get upgrades and hopefully more customers."

Paddington smiled, but didn't say anything. He slowed when a motorcycle cut in front of them, then flashed his lights until the cyclist pulled over. Rather than stop and ticket him, Paddington kept going.

The D.C.I. tapped his brakes at the next stop sign. "I should have come to the same conclusion as you," he admitted, "about the kidnapping and murder. But I was looking at Clark Partridge as the linch pin."

"And I was focused on the renovations and who

might want to ruin the construction and dredging. I thought Weymouth—"

"He was one of my suspects, too, in the first few hours. But I cut him pretty fast. He's been keeping his nose clean ever since I arrested him the last time for vandalism. I just couldn't see him for this." Paddington drummed his fingers against the steering wheel. "Doesn't mean I won't arrest him again, though. When the dredging starts back up, if he and his Gladiators cause trouble, I'll pinch him. The jail ought to have plenty of empty cells by then."

"And then I wondered about someone in the Draghici clan…maybe Stefan. One hundred and fifty thousand pounds would set his family up for a while. Michael figured it could be Esma."

"Never looked at them," Paddington admitted. "Oh, a lot of folks around here think all Gypsies are thieves, and I wouldn't put it past the Draghicis for doing something illegal, but I never believed they'd craft something like a kidnapping scheme. They're the direct kind. And I believe they really might be entitled to that gold."

"If it exists," Molly said.

They passed Blackpool's only London plane tree, a one-hundred-and-sixty-foot giant that shaded practically an entire block. The tree was said to be as old as the town itself.

Paddington grimaced. "You're quite the sleuth,

Molly Graham. Maybe you should have followed in your uncle's stealthy footsteps. Maybe you still can."

"I've never considered myself a sleuth, really. I just…I dunno. I like puzzles. Or, rather, I hate them. I hate to see something unfinished. It's an itch, and I have to keep scratching until the itch goes away." She stunned herself with that admission. "I guess I just can't leave anything unresolved. Like with the Green Gladiators. I'm going to have to find a way to get them to believe the studies that were done on the harbor and the silt, lay it all out for them again, bring in an ecologist if I have to. I want the issue settled, and to their satisfaction, too."

"Everything in its place, I suppose." Paddington glanced at her, a serious expression on his weary face. "Some things just don't settle, Molly. Like Weymouth. He's a driven man, tortures himself about his causes and what he sees as hurtful to the world. He's got blinders on, and while you might convince some of his followers that all of this is for the good of Blackpool and the fishes and lobsters out in the bay, you'll not convince him. He has his mind made up."

He pulled into a driveway, right up to the bumper of a little yellow car, which wouldn't be able to leave now.

"So, if you were looking at the harbor as the motive to the kidnapping, Molly, what made you switch your thinking to Rosamund?"

Molly got out and followed Paddington up the front

steps to the porch that wrapped around half the old stately house.

"Something Atkinson said in your interview room."

"Yes, I'd gathered you were watching…the way you burst in on me like that. Don't ever do it again."

She decided not to tell him that Sergeant Krebs had let her in, not wanting to risk getting the woman in trouble.

"Atkinson mentioned Clark Partridge having a girl-friend." Molly paused when Paddington rang the bell and discovered it didn't work. He rapped loudly on the door. "And Rosamund said she was in London with a boyfriend, yet just a little while ago she told me she didn't have one. So I thought Partridge might have been it, and then with him dead…"

"No more boyfriend." Paddington knocked again, made a huffing sound and tried the knob. "Rosamund always did have a reputation for favoring what they call bad boys. Her father fretted over that."

"Besides, Rosamund had called him Party, just like Atkinson did." Molly suddenly felt a profound sorrow for Dennis Carteret. In jail, reduced to thievery over a daughter he cherished dearly…and who was quite possibly a murderer. The man's life was ruined. "Another thing bothered me—she never seemed upset enough about her father's situation. Some, but not enough."

Paddington tried the door and found it unlocked,

though he had to give the old wood a shove to get it to open.

"Keep your distance and mind your manners, Molly. I should have my head examined, letting you tag along. Damn, I should have called for backup, at least brought Sergeant Krebs. And I should be telling you to wait out in the car, you know."

"I know," Molly said.

"D.C.I. Paddington," Rosamund said. She was at the top of a sweeping staircase just past the entryway, fingers touching the highly polished walnut banister. An assortment of suitcases stood behind her and a bag was slung across her back. "I wondered when you would figure things out."

CHAPTER TWENTY-SEVEN

PADDINGTON RESTED HIS HAND on his gun holster and after a moment unsnapped it.

"I'm not armed," she said. "There's no gun in the house. Dad doesn't own one."

"Come on down, Rosamund. Let's you and I have a talk."

She started descending the stairs. It looked to Molly as if she'd been crying…but over what? The crumpled paper bag that had held her father's shirt was on its side on the landing, open and empty. Faintly, Molly heard the sound of a washing machine hit its spin cycle.

"I really didn't mean for there to be trouble," Rosamund said. She paused halfway down and glanced at the wall. It held an array of large family photographs and paintings displayed in ornate and expensive-looking frames. Rosamund seemed to be staring at one taken in a photography studio, judging by its backdrop of swirling pale gray-green. It showed the Carteret family, mother holding a baby in a pink blanket and father beaming down, smiling.

Next to it was another photograph, not as large, of mother and daughter. Rosamund looked to be about five or six in it, a little white dog at her feet. Her mother was noticeably pregnant. Rosamund reached out and touched the image of the dog, then bounced to the bottom of the steps and stopped in front of Paddington.

"So…what was it?" she asked, putting on a face like a petulant school girl. "What did I do wrong? Not cover my tracks well enough, apparently. What made you realize I'd turned Party into brown bread?"

Molly's mouth dropped open. She'd realized back at the station that Rosamund was likely the murderer, but had she heard right? Did the girl just confess? Paddington hadn't even asked her a question.

"You and Clark Partridge were together in London," he began.

"So some sod tattled on us. Loftus? Party's chum? Party probably told him where we were going, where we were staying. Old Lofty liked to keep tabs on Party, you know." She sashayed past Paddington and gave Molly a wink, then settled into an overstuffed chair in the parlor. "Join me? I'd put on some tea, but I suppose we don't have time for that."

"No, we don't." Paddington took a seat opposite her. Molly stayed in the doorway where she could watch from a respectful distance.

"Who came up with the kidnapping idea? You, or was it Clark?"

Rosamund snorted. "Party was a berk. Oh, don't get me wrong, the lad was a rabbit in bed, and Dad couldn't stand him. Caught me and him together last year. Mad as a box of frogs, Dad was. So…two counts in Party's favor. Party said he loved me, but I didn't buy it. I was just a Page Three girl to him. Get what I mean?"

"So the kidnapping idea—"

"Was all mine." Rosamund wiped at her eyes again. "I'm smart, you know. Dad shipped me off to the best schools…shipped me off a couple of times."

"To a boarding school when you were very young, if I recall," Paddington said. He hunched forward, elbows on his knees, and dropped his head, his hat falling off into his waiting hands. He looked up at her. "Sent you away shortly after—"

"After Mum died. It was a good school. I was top of the class. Gifted, they called me."

"Gifted enough to concoct a believable kidnapping ploy," Paddington said.

Molly heard the washer stop and saw Rosamund look in the direction of the far doorway.

"I should get that," she said. "Toss it in the dryer so it won't get all mildewy-smelling. They do that, shirts, if you let them sit in the washer too long."

"Later," Paddington said. "I want to hear about the kidnapping."

"Should I be calling a barrister?"

"You've every right to do that."

She shrugged, the gesture sending her overly

large blouse off one shoulder. "Maybe I'll use Dad's barrister."

"Would you like to call for him now?"

"No."

For several moments the silence in the room was thick. Paddington watched Rosamund, and her gaze flitted from picture to picture, to the Oriental rug on the floor, then back to the D.C.I. Molly heard a car pass by out on the street and an angry bird squawk at something. Another car drove by, then one stopped nearby and a door slammed.

"I wanted to get away," Rosamund said finally. "I wanted to go…somewhere. I don't know…Ireland maybe. Maybe farther, China or New Zealand. Go somewhere and start new, a big city, and never look back. Someplace exciting. This rural life is a snooze. I needed more glamor."

"You needed money for that."

"I have money, but it wasn't enough. I didn't have a job, and I wasn't about to get one around here. Nothing fun, nothing that would pay well. And Dad, there's no way he would've handed over enough dosh for me to have a long-term fling. He always wanted to keep me close, so controlling."

"But you knew he had money."

She rotated her head. "Duh. Just look at this place. Filled with expensive things, antiques from his grand-dad. A restaurant by the docks, a boat…a big one."

"Named *Rosamund's Dream*," Paddington said.

"Except boating was never my dream," she retorted sharply. "My dream was to live large somewhere else. But, yeah, I knew he had money. I just assumed he had enough sitting around that he could pay the ransom with it."

"You gave him, what—"

"Clark made the call and disguised his voice. Clark gave Dad twenty-four hours to come up with the dosh."

"But he didn't have that much 'sitting around' as you put it."

She pouted. "No. I never imagined he'd trundle off with a big chunk of the harbor fund, and drag that sod Percy into the muck with him. I never meant for Dad to get hurt. Well, not hurt so much."

Molly thought Rosamund had folded in upon herself. She looked small and childlike and terribly vulnerable.

"I love Dad, at least a little," she said after Paddington had let the silence settle again. "I really didn't mean for all of this to happen. I should've covered my tracks better. Shouldn't have gacked Party…at least not where he could be found. God, but I was stupid about that, wasn't I?"

Paddington didn't reply. He sat quietly.

"Party…he was never keen on the idea to begin with."

"No? Why was that?"

Another shrug, the blouse slipped farther down her

shoulder and she demurely straightened it. "He'd had some run-ins with you before. Not you, specifically, but the Blackpool constables, with a Mick cop, too, when he was on a holiday in Dublin. Party didn't want to get in any more trouble. He even tried to talk me out of the whole thing, this kidnapping. But I wasn't listening. I was thinking about China or New Zealand, even had a vague notion about Argentina, but they have too many earthquakes there."

"You convinced Clark Partridge to go through with it." Paddington hadn't posed it as a question.

"Took some doing, but yeah. I told him Dad could well afford it…or so I thought. I'd even considered asking for more—two, three, four hundred thousand. That would have been sweet. Party said that was crazy, though. Said I was pushing all the envelopes in the world and that Dad would have to bring the police in for sure. In the end, I got him to make the call. We were sneaky, buying one of those disposable cells like you see them do in the movies."

"And your father believed Clark and got the money."

"Clark was real familiar with some of the walking trails by the cliffs, so he picked a spot where he could hide from the road and Dad wouldn't see him. I'd dropped him off there and came back later."

"And you killed him because you didn't want to share the money."

Rosamund hit her thigh with her open hand. "No!

That wasn't it at all. I'd never intended to share the money. Oh, I might've given him enough to pay off the gambling debt he owed Lofty, but that would've been it. Party knew that, knew it was all for me."

"Then why did you slit his throat?"

Molly sucked in a breath, waiting for Rosamund to wise up and ask for a barrister before incriminating herself.

"It was nice that night. I came to get Party and I parked on the access road so nobody would see me. That time of night, not a soul was around, not that a lot of people walk that trail anyway. I should've pushed him off. I tried to, but he was stronger than me. He fought for his life. In the end I just took a knife across his throat…and that wasn't easy, either. He was trying to get away from me. But it was dark, and he tripped. If he hadn't fallen, he might've got away."

Molly gripped the wainscoting, mesmerized and horrified at the same time.

"Party was having third thoughts, you see. When he was holding that satchel filled with money, he looked at me and said it was wrong. He dropped it on the trail and told me it was all mine and he wanted no piece of it, that he'd find another way to pay Lofty back. Of course it was all mine, but I was still thinking about paying off his debt, just to be nice. But then I realized how stupid he was and I thought he might, you know, talk about the whole thing. To Lofty or to Atkinson. I was afraid word might somehow get to the police."

Paddington nodded knowingly. "You'd brought a knife with you."

Premeditation, Molly thought.

"Just in case. I'd been wondering if I was going to have to gack him, and I thought I should be prepared in case. I was always good at dissecting. Science was my best subject."

"The knife—"

"Just a steak knife from the set in the kitchen. Stainless. You can see the slot in the drawer where it goes. The set cost a pretty penny. I threw the knife away after. It was all bloody. Tossed it off the cliff, like I should've tossed Party's body but where he'd fallen was hard to get to. I probably would've got away with it, wouldn't I? If you hadn't found the body?"

Paddington didn't answer that.

"I mean, you wouldn't have figured me to fake my own kidnapping, right? You wouldn't have thought sweet, petite Rosamund would do something so horrid. I went back to the trail, but you were already there." She shrugged. "In the light I would've been able to see better, drag him off the cliff. Should've tried to do it in the dark, but I was afraid I might fall. So I came home a few days later, found out Dad was in jail. I'd only returned because I wanted to pick up some things before I moved away."

"The money…" Paddington prompted.

"I had to act like I didn't know anything about the kidnapping, pretend to be the perfect daughter. Great drama coach, I had. Any road, I stashed the money upstairs."

"It's still there?"

"Most all of it. I spent a little on new clothes. It's in the big red suitcase at the top of the stairs."

Paddington turned and studied a photograph. It was the one Molly had looked at when she'd come here. A very young Rosamund sat on her mother's knee, a small white dog in her lap.

"Fluffy," Rosamund said. "My dog's name was Fluffy."

"You've done horrid things before, Rosamund."

"That was a long while ago, D.C.I."

"I wasn't here then," Paddington said.

"I was only six. Six and a half, actually."

"There's a record of it, the incident, down at the station. I saw it when I arrested your father. Just a simple incident report. But it was more than that, wasn't it?"

"I was only six," she repeated, this time with a little fire in her voice. "Six and a half. Nobody ever proved anything."

"Didn't your father send you away to the boarding school right after? Your first boarding school, wasn't it?"

Molly's fingernails sank into the soft wood of the wainscoting.

"I didn't want Mum to have another child. She didn't need to be sharing her attention. She should've waited for me to get a little older. Dad believed me when I said the dog did it, tripped her at the top of the stairs. But then he made me give the dog up. I hated him for that."

"The dog didn't trip your mother."

"Just a push," Rosamund whined. "She wasn't supposed to die. Just the baby in her belly."

Molly was beginning to feel faint.

"I heard there were troubles at the boarding school."

"Nothing terrible," Rosamund answered. She sat up straight and looked at the back doorway again. "I really should be getting that shirt out of the washer. Mildew, you know."

"That's why you were moved around," Paddington continued. "Problems at different schools. Counselors, therapists. Your dad spent quite a bit of money on you."

"I had to work a lot of things out," she said. "Now, about that shirt."

"Someone will tend to it later." Paddington stood. "Let's go down to the station."

"I should probably call a barrister from there, shouldn't I?"

"I think that would be a good idea."

CHAPTER TWENTY-EIGHT

THE SILENCE IN Paddington's car was uncomfortable. Rosamund was in the back. The D.C.I. hadn't hand-cuffed her, but he had searched her to make sure she indeed didn't have any weapons. The suitcase with the money in it was locked in the trunk.

Rosamund was mentally ill, Molly realized, and probably should have been committed to care rather than bounced from one boarding school to the next. Partridge might still be alive, and Carteret would never have stolen from the harbor fund.

Perhaps the court might force her into an institution where she'd finally get the help she needed. In any event, she would be out of Blackpool.

Molly had helped solve the case. She should feel elated, she should be patting herself on the back. She should plan a celebration with Michael tonight and go to that fancy restaurant with its linen tablecloths and wonderful wine list. Instead, all she felt was despair. Dennis Carteret was in jail, headed to prison, and his daughter would be following.

There was no happy ending to this mystery.

The radio crackled. Paddington turned up the

volume and punched a button on the console. "Say that again, please."

"I said there's been a shooting at the Crowe Mansion."

"Can't pin that one on me," Rosamund said. "You're my alibi. I was with the two of you the whole time."

Molly leaned forward as much as the seat belt allowed so she could hear the dispatcher better.

Paddington spoke into a microphone on the dash. "Give me the details."

"Three constables are on the scene, plus Sergeant Krebs. It seems Aleister Crowe caught a burglar or a trespasser—we're still working that out. The man had broken into the manor, but Aleister shot him before he got too far. Someone's bringing Aleister to the station now."

"Is the…trespasser, burglar…dead?"

"No, sir. But he's in a bad way. The ambulance just took him to the hospital."

"Got a name on him?"

Molly heard paper shuffling and the *click-click-click* of a computer keyboard.

"Wallace, sir. The man's name is Rohan Wallace. Sergeant Krebs said he's a laborer from the marina. Definitely not from around here. The ambulance crew doubts he'll make it."

Molly's chest grew tight and her heart rose into her throat.

"Hurry," she whispered.

"You don't have to tell me that, Molly." Paddington flicked a switch, the siren and lights came on, and he expertly sped down Blackpool's tight streets toward the police station.

"Wallace is a friend of yours, right?"

"Yes. Well, more Michael's than mine." She pulled the mobile from her pocket and looked at the screen. Three more missed calls since she'd turned it off, all in the past few minutes, and all from Michael.

Paddington hadn't rolled the car to a complete stop when Molly unhooked the seat belt and rushed out.

"I'll meet you at the hospital," he shouted to her as she darted toward her car, scrambled inside it and bolted off to the hospital.

She found Michael in the waiting area outside the casualty ward—what the Blackpool hospital called its emergency room.

Merciful Angels Hospital, though two decades old, was considered one of the town's newest buildings. Prior to that Blackpool had had to rush patients to nearby towns for advanced care. It was the smallest hospital Molly had been in, but the town was proud of it, and the doctors were said to be first-rate.

"They bagged him, Molly."

"What?" Molly pictured a coroner zipping up a black vinyl bag around Rohan's bloody body.

"In the ambulance," Michael said. "They had to bag him—had to hook an ambu bag onto his mask and pump it to help him breathe."

She exhaled. "He's not dead."

"Not yet, but I overheard a nurse say it looks bleak, that he was trying to crump on them."

Michael dropped into a plastic chair and put his head in his hands. Molly stood in front of him and gently touched the back of his neck. "I'm sorry," she said. The words were inadequate. "I know he's your friend."

"Yes, he's my friend. But he's still a mystery. I couldn't even give them the name of a family member to call." Michael's voice was muted, his face still aimed at the tile floor.

Molly hated hospitals. Sure, there were moments of joy, such as the birth of a baby. But more often it was a place of intense grief, a palpable mass of fear and uncertainty and desperation. The smells didn't help, the disinfectant, the cloying scent of visitors' perfumes and flowers on the counter at the nurse's station. The sounds made things worse—the *clackety-clack* of wheels on gurneys, the soft bleeping of machines recording vital signs and the hiss of respirators.

"If he makes it out of this, Molly, I'm going to get him some fresh ackee. I'll make Coffey's special-order it, and Iris can fix ackee and cod again.

"I tried to find him," Michael went on. "I looked around the harbor a few times, and went to his flat. People in the neighboring apartments said he was coming and going at odd hours. I should have tried harder."

"It's not your fault," Molly reassured him, "and not your responsibility."

A nurse walked by, the sound of her tread causing Michael to glance up. "Any word?"

She stopped and regarded the pair. "Who are you waiting for news on?"

"Rohan Wallace, the man in the casualty room?"

"Are you a relative?"

"Uh, no. I don't know if he has any family. Certainly not in Blackpool. He's from Jamaica."

"I'm sorry, we can only release information to the family." She walked away, consulting a clipboard as she went.

Michael's head dropped back into his hands. Molly sat next to him and placed a hand on his knee.

Two hours later a doctor emerged, mask untied and hanging against his scrubs like a bib. There was blood on the front of his shirt, and when he tugged his cap off, Molly saw that his hair was plastered to his head with sweat.

"You Michael Graham?"

Michael stood and nodded. "Rohan doesn't have family here in town. But I'm a friend."

The doctor looked grim and Molly gripped the arms of the chair, waiting for the bad news.

"The hospital has a policy that we only talk to relatives."

"I don't think he has—"

"D.C.I. Paddington is trying to contact his family,

I've been told. He's going through the police department in Kingston. But with the time difference, it could
be a while."

"Can't you tell me anything?"

The doctor wiped his hands against his hips. "I can't
say if he's going to make it. He lost a lot of blood. He
was shot in the chest. It missed his heart, but punctured
a lung. His left lung collapsed. We got the bullet and
patched him up."

"Can I see him?"

"You can look in on him." The doctor motioned
to the nurse who'd walked by earlier. "What room is
Wallace in?"

"Your friend is in a coma in intensive care," the
nurse said. "Down that way and to your right. They
won't let you in, but there's a big window. If you're a
religious man, Mr. Graham, you might want to pray
for him."

CHAPTER TWENTY-NINE

MOLLY AND MICHAEL were met by Paddington, Aleister and Aubrey in the waiting area of the intensive care ward.

Aleister stepped forward. "Your friend, Michael…" He motioned with his cane like an orchestra conductor waved a baton. "I'm suing him. I'm pressing charges. He trespassed! Broke into my home."

"Shhhh!" a frumpy nurse at the station scolded him. "Keep your voice down."

"This isn't a library," Aleister said. Still, he lowered his voice. "I shot him."

"Then why haven't you been arrested?" Molly demanded. "Why aren't you in jail?"

"Nothing to charge him with," Paddington said. He stayed back, face pressed against a window. "It was his property, and apparently Rohan Wallace was trespassing. Moreover, according to Aleister and Aubrey, he refused to leave."

"He threatened me," Aleister continued. "He raised his fist, and I shot him. I didn't kill him."

"Yet," Michael said.

Aleister puffed out his chest and pulled in his neck,

giving Michael and Molly his best vulture glare. "I will sue him if he survives. I'll press every charge I can. My manor is sacrosanct. He was uninvited." He nodded at Paddington, who wasn't looking at him, then at Michael and Molly. "I've business to attend to elsewhere. Michael, I hope your friend survives so Paddington can arrest him."

Aubrey followed him down the hall.

"I'm sorry about your friend, Michael," Paddington remarked after the Crowes had disappeared. "And I'm sorry I couldn't arrest Aleister. That will change if your friend comes out of his coma and has a different story to tell. I'm compelled to go along with Aleister's version until that happens."

"But you will investigate?" The question came from Molly. She joined Paddington at the window. On the other side, Rohan lay stretched out on a hospital bed, a peach-colored blanket pulled up to his waist and thick bandages around his chest. He was hooked up to three machines. One monitored the slow but steady beat of his heart. He was breathing on his own, but he had a tube with oxygen stuck in his nose. His eyes were closed and his dreadlocks were splayed across the pillow. She shuddered. He looked so feeble surrounded by all the equipment.

"I'll investigate. I'm reasonably good at it." He gave her a nudge. "But I might need a little help from Blackpool's resident detective."

Molly smiled.

They ate in the hospital's tiny cafeteria, the three of them picking at a meal of chicken, rice and applesauce.

"What do you really know of Rohan Wallace?" Paddington directed the question to Michael.

"I met him by chance a few months back—I liked him right off," Michael said. "He didn't tell me much about himself, and to be honest, I didn't press. What do you know?"

"More than you, apparently. I'd thought about mentioning this before, but I didn't want to intrude and ruin your friendship. It's a man's own business who he makes friends with."

Michael waited for Paddington to continue.

"From what I gather, he hasn't been in Jamaica for a few years. He's been traveling around Europe, doing odd jobs to get by. I'm convinced he's in Blackpool for the gold. In fact, my sources say he'd been asking about the treasure well before he ran into you. And I understand the two of you have been working pretty hard at finding it lately."

Michael nodded. "Rohan and I built a model of Blackpool as it existed about a hundred years ago. He was quick to help me with it. I guess I should have realized his eagerness stemmed from something deeper."

"He's known to police. He's had a few scrapes with the law in Manchester, Belfast, Toledo and Kingston. Nothing serious, but enough to give him a record. A disorderly, two shoplifting charges, a minor breaking-and-entering when he was a teen. Nothing in the past couple of years, though."

"So he might have been going straight," Michael said.

"Could be. But this…this I think might have been something more. He's after the Blackpool treasure, and broke into the Crowe mansion looking for something. That project you said he was helping you with—"

"My miniature town?"

"Maybe something about your project gave him an idea. Something about one of Charles Crowe's build-ings. And that led him to the Crowe mansion."

"If the treasure even exists," Molly said in a hushed voice.

It was dark when the trio left the hospital, after taking a last look at Rohan, who lay hooked up to the machines, still in a coma.

CHAPTER THIRTY

BACK AT HOME, Michael tugged Molly upstairs.

"Good night, Iris," he said as he passed her in the entryway.

"And how was your day?" she called.

"Long," Michael said. "We'll tell you about it tomorrow."

Molly had to hurry to keep up with his longer legs. "That was a bit short."

"I know. I'll apologize in the morning. Come, there's something you have to see. It can't wait. Honest."

"Right now? I'm so tired. Exhausted, actually." *And beaten down by all the horrible things that happened today,* she wanted to add. "I'd like to take a long, hot bath, with bubbles up to my chin."

"You'll have time for that in a bit. C'mon." He practically dragged her up to his third-floor office.

"This is why I was trying to find Rohan...or, rather, one of the reasons. We'd worked so hard on all these little buildings. And I should have realized then...well, I did realize that there was something more to him. Rohan fit everything together like a master builder."

The words tumbled fast from Michael's mouth, some of them running together.

"His buildings were more precise than mine, and it didn't take him quite so long to build them. He knew to mark doors and windows and how to make everything perfectly to scale. I started doing the same, or as best as I could. And I redid the first ones I'd built."

"And all of this by hand? You didn't use the computer?"

He pushed open the door to his office and tugged her inside. "All by hand. For some reason I thought I needed to be able to touch them."

"Michael, I really don't want to hear about your treasure hunt." Molly sucked in a breath. She was on the verge of tears, the events of the day threatening to overwhelm her. She touched her stomach; it had started to whir like a blender again and she feared it might reject what little hospital cafeteria food she'd shoved into it.

"I know, I know," Michael said. "Now isn't a good time for this. But it can't wait. I can't wait. This has something to do with why my friend's in a coma at the hospital."

"Okay, show me your little Blackpool."

Michael held out his hand, and she took it, folding her fingers inside his. He drew her close, and his lips brushed her forehead. "I love you, Molly Graham."

"I love you, Michael Graham."

He kissed her, and then he took her to the table,

where a balsa-wood Blackpool was spread out on a map with carefully labeled streets.

"I finished it. All the buildings are now accurate models of the ones in the town. But it's more than that, I can feel it. It's a puzzle."

"This is a puzzle?"

"Well, of course. The whole notion of a fabulous treasure hunt—"

"—if the gold exists—"

"—is one big game. This model is the key to everything—the treasure, the *Seaclipse,* Charles Crowe."

He picked up the buildings one by one, turning them this way and that and adjusting the roofs. "I just have to figure out how. It could be the only thing that saves Rohan's life."

Michael sagged and Molly put her arms around him. "Come to bed, love. We've solved enough mysteries today. Charles Crowe and his secrets will have their day soon…."

* * * * *

REQUEST YOUR FREE BOOKS!

2 FREE NOVELS
FROM THE SUSPENSE COLLECTION
PLUS 2 FREE GIFTS!

YES! Please send me 2 FREE novels from the Suspense Collection and my 2 FREE gifts (gifts are worth about $10). After receiving them, if I don't wish to receive any more books, I can return the shipping statement marked "cancel." If I don't cancel, I will receive 4 brand-new novels every month and be billed just $5.74 per book in the U.S. or $6.24 per book in Canada. That's a saving of at least 28% off the cover price. It's quite a bargain! Shipping and handling is just 50¢ per book in the U.S. and 75¢ per book in Canada.* I understand that accepting the 2 free books and gifts places me under no obligation to buy anything. I can always return a shipment and cancel at any time. Even if I never buy another book, the two free books and gifts are mine to keep forever.

191/391 MDN FDDH

Name	(PLEASE PRINT)

Address	Apt. #

City	State/Prov.	Zip/Postal Code

Signature (if under 18, a parent or guardian must sign)

Mail to the **Reader Service:**
IN U.S.A.: P.O. Box 1867, Buffalo, NY 14240-1867
IN CANADA: P.O. Box 609, Fort Erie, Ontario L2A 5X3

Not valid for current subscribers to the Suspense Collection
or the Romance/Suspense Collection.

Want to try two free books from another line?
Call 1-800-873-8635 or visit www.ReaderService.com.

* Terms and prices subject to change without notice. Prices do not include applicable taxes. Sales tax applicable in N.Y. Canadian residents will be charged applicable taxes. Offer not valid in Quebec. This offer is limited to one order per household. All orders subject to credit approval. Credit or debit balances in a customer's account(s) may be offset by any other outstanding balance owed by or to the customer. Please allow 4 to 6 weeks for delivery. Offer available while quantities last.

Your Privacy—The Reader Service is committed to protecting your privacy. Our Privacy Policy is available online at www.ReaderService.com or upon request from the Reader Service.

We make a portion of our mailing list available to reputable third parties that offer products we believe may interest you. If you prefer that we not exchange your name with third parties, or if you wish to clarify or modify your communication preferences, please visit us at www.ReaderService.com/consumerchoice or write to us at Reader Service Preference Service, P.O. Box 9062, Buffalo, NY 14269. Include your complete name and address.

Start your Best Body today with these top 3 nutrition tips!

1. **SHOP THE PERIMETER OF THE GROCERY STORE:** The good stuff—fruits, veggies, lean proteins and dairy—always line the outer edges of the store. When you veer into the center aisles, you enter the temptation zone, where the unhealthy foods live.

2. **WATCH PORTION SIZES:** Most portion sizes in restaurants are nearly twice the size of a true serving and at home, it's easy to "clean your plate." Use these easy serving guidelines:
   - Protein: the palm of your hand
   - Grains or Fruit: a cup of your hand
   - Veggies: the palm of two open hands

3. **USE THE RAINBOW RULE FOR PRODUCE:** Your produce drawers should be filled with every color of fruits and vegetables. The greater the variety, the more vitamins and other nutrients you add to your diet.

Find these and many more helpful tips in

YOUR BEST BODY NOW

by

TOSCA RENO

WITH STACY BAKER

Bestselling Author of THE EAT-CLEAN DIET®

Available wherever books are sold!

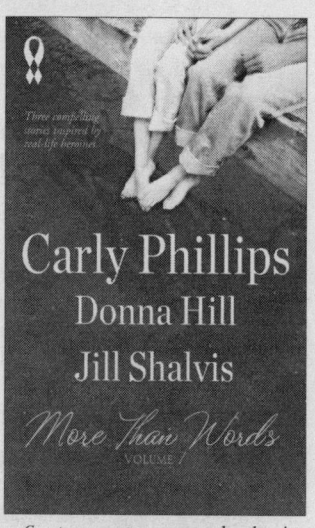

PAMELA CALLOW

Lawyer Kate Lange has survived the darkest period of her troubled life, and the wounds are still raw. Now she's been handed a case that seems unwinnable—defending her boss, high-profile lawyer Randall Barrett. A prosecutor's dream suspect, Randall was cuckolded by his ex-wife, and could not control his temper, arguing bitterly with the victim the previous day in full view of the children.

Kate finds herself enmeshed in a family fractured by doubt. As Kate races to stay a step ahead of the prosecution, a silent predator is waiting to deal the final blow—and this time his victim is Randall's daughter.

INDEFENSIBLE

Available wherever books are sold.